BRUTAL CLAIM

PLANET OF KINGS BOOK TWO

LEE SAVINO
TABITHA BLACK

SILVERWOOD PRESS

Copyright © November 2021 by Lee Savino, Tabitha Black and Silverwood Press

---

WARNING: Contains dark themes and elements which may be triggering for some people. Proceed with caution!

This book is a work of fiction. The names, characters, places, and incidents are products of the writers' imagination or have been used fictitiously and are not to be construed as real. Any resemblance to persons, living or dead, actual events, locales or organizations is entirely coincidental.

WARNING: The unauthorized reproduction of this work is illegal. Criminal copyright infringement is investigated by the FBI and is punishable by up to 5 years in federal prison and a fine of $250,000.

All rights reserved. With the exception of quotes used in reviews, this book may not be reproduced or used in whole or in part by any means existing without written permission from the authors.

This book contains descriptions of many dark sexual practices, but this is a work of fiction and, as such, should not be used in any way as a guide. The author and publisher will not be responsible for any loss, harm, injury, or death resulting from use of the information contained within. In other words, don't try this at home, folks!

BRUTAL CLAIM

Aurus:

The High King of Ulfaria needs no introduction. What I need is an Omega.
And now, I've found one. Kim. She is small and perfect, as I knew she would be.
I will demand her obedience, then I will give her the perfect nest and allow her to bear my heirs.
She vows to defy me, but one way or another, she will submit.

Kim:

Hold. My. Beer.

ONE

Kim

SOMETHING EPIC MUST HAVE HAPPENED. The problem is, I don't remember what it was.

My mouth tastes like rotting compost, there's a roaring in my ears, and tiny icepicks are being driven repeatedly into my temples.

In other words, I feel like shit.

I try to crack my eyes open, but the sudden blinding pain forces me to close them again. Where am I? What happened?

Probing my memory, I try to work out where and when I was last awake. No dice. Come to think of it, there are more holes in my recollection than there are actual memories.

Last night must have been one insane party.

I try opening my eyes again—carefully this time. Blinking furiously, I slowly get accustomed to the light. It's not as bright as I first thought it would be.

The ceiling looks... unusual. Ornate. High. Very, very high.

Where the fuck am I?

Forcing myself slowly from a prone to a sitting position, I clutch at my pounding temples, blink some more, and look around.

I must still be asleep. Or unconscious. In any case, I'm dreaming.

There is no way in hell I'm actually where I seem to be.

In a harem.

The space is enormous—easily the size of my old school gym. There are ornate, scrolled columns, elaborate cornices, and sheer, wispy fabrics in a rainbow of shades. Pastel-colored glowing orbs float everywhere, seemingly by magic, bathing the whole place in soothing, pretty light. There's a gentle floral scent, contrasting sharply with the gross taste in my mouth. The whole place is like something out of *1001 Nights*.

Complete with the women.

There are maybe a dozen or so, all dressed in gossamer, flowing gowns, and glittering with golden jewelry. But as I look closer, I realize there's something really strange about them.

They don't look... human.

They're tall—the shortest is over six feet, at the very least. And their skin... is that body paint? Green, lilac, blue, bronze—their faces, their hands, their feet—they seem to come in as wide an array of colors as the curtains cascading down the walls. They're tattooed all over—as far as I can tell—with strikingly contrasting colors, and they all have long, brightly-hued hair in different shades to their skin.

What in the everlasting fuck?

One of them notices me, and comes over. She moves in

a weird way. More gliding than walking. As she approaches, she calls something over her shoulder, and the sound of it makes the hair on the backs of my arms stand up.

It's not English. It's not any language I've ever heard. Not even close. A series of clicks and mewls and long, drawn out vowels...

... and yet I can understand it, clear as day.

"She's awake!"

Somehow, this is starting to feel too realistic to be a dream. Frozen in place, I can do nothing but wait as the strange woman approaches me.

She's stunning up close. Her skin is the softest shade of blue, and her long, wavy hair is a deep mauve. Her eyes are almost feline and when she blinks, I notice her long, purple lashes.

"Welcome to Aurum," she says.

"What?" I feel like I'm speaking English, but there's something inside my head that twists my tongue and makes gobbledygook come out instead.

Am I really speaking her freaking language right now? *How?*

"Aurum," she repeats, as if this is just a normal day, and dazed, confused women appear in her home all the time.

"What's that?"

"Ulfaria."

Maybe we're not speaking the same language after all.

"Lenah," another voice says, and I realize I'm surrounded by the women now. They're all peering at me with a combination of awe and curiosity. "She is not from here. She does not know the names of our kingdoms and planet. She will be confused, as the mage said."

All that, I understood. Not that it lessened my gigantic

freakout one bit. Kingdoms? Planet? Confused is a damn understatement.

"Huh," Lenah—I presume—says. She leans a little closer to me. "What is your name?"

What *is* my name?

The low-key anxiety I'd been experiencing up until this moment becomes a full-body shiver of panic as I realize I'm struggling to answer this most basic question. Not only do I not know where I am or how I got here, apparently I don't know *who* I am, either.

"Omega," another girl supplies helpfully.

I shake my head. It's definitely not that.

"Omega," Lenah agrees. "Once the serum has started to work. They said it would take a little while."

Serum?

Deciding I've had enough, I pinch the inside of my wrist so hard, it makes me gasp.

As one, the women all lean back and gasp too.

Aaand I'm still here. Not dreaming, then.

Fuck. Fuck. Fuck.

I clear my throat, wondering what to say. I have so many questions. *Take me to your leader* would probably be pushing it, but there's actually a tiny part of me that's wondering whether I'm not just not at home, I'm not actually on Earth right now.

But that's just insane. Not feasible. Not realistic. Not possible.

Kim! The name comes to me in a flash, and I recognize it as mine. Thank god. It's a start. I clear my throat.

"My name is Kim. Could somebody please," I begin slowly, "explain to me where I am, and why I'm here. This is Earth, right? We're still on Earth?" May as well get the big one out of the way first.

The second girl, who's a gorgeous shade of turquoise, gives me a look of unadulterated pity. "No," she says. "This is Ulfaria. Earth is *your* planet. Ulfaria is ours."

"We're on another planet?" My voice catches on the last word. I can barely believe what I'm saying—in an alien language, no less.

"Yes. This is Aurum, the biggest kingdom on Ulfaria."

"Why," I swallow, "did you bring me here?" At least we're having a conversation I can comprehend now, even if I'm struggling to believe it.

"For King Aurus," Lenah takes over from the turquoise girl. "He needs an Omega. You will be his Omega."

So much for comprehending the conversation. "I'm not an Omega," I say. "I'm a human. I'm a human, and I would like to leave." Where I will go, I'm not sure, but anywhere other than here would be preferable. The harem setting, the beautiful women, and now talk of giving me to some king is making me seriously nervous.

What's worse than waking up on an alien planet?

Waking up on an alien planet and being told you're going to be some alien king's plaything.

"You were given serum," the turquoise girl says. "It will make you into an Omega."

My throat constricts and I start to choke. "Could I have something to drink?" I manage, in between splutters.

One of the other girls glides away, then returns and hands me a shiny bejeweled goblet filled with a dark liquid. I gulp it down greedily. It doesn't taste too bad—a little sweet with a hint of spice. It's refreshing, and takes away the horrible taste in my mouth. "More, please?" I entreat her, holding the empty goblet out like I'm begging for alms.

While the girl goes to fetch another drink for me, I take a breath, trying to stay as calm as possible.

"My name is Kim," I say, pointing to my chest.

"Kim," the women chorus, as one. It's eerie.

"I'm Juno," the turquoise girl says. "We need to get you ready."

"Ready for what?" Maybe I shouldn't have asked.

"To meet King Aurus. He is eager to see you."

"No shit," I mutter, and rise slowly, unsteadily to my feet. I'm handed the goblet again and drain it once more, wondering whether they have alcohol on this planet. I'm certainly feeling light-headed.

The girls all look at each other, then Lenah once again takes charge. "Undress," she says bossily, "the bath has already been drawn."

I'm torn. I feel sticky with fear, and being in water has always soothed and grounded me, but I'm not about to be *prepared for the king* like some sacrificial virgin. "Show me where the bath is," I say, "and I'll bathe myself."

Lenah lets out a snort, and a couple of the other girls giggle. "We will bathe you," she says firmly, and the next moment, both my arms have been seized and I'm being dragged along.

I'm at least a foot shorter than most of these women, and slender, but I don't make it easy for them, digging in my heels and spitting curses at them all the way.

They seem unfazed as they haul me to a door I hadn't noticed, hidden behind a curtain. It glides open as if by invisible command, and then my unceremonious journey continues until we arrive at a huge bronze tub, complete with gently steaming scented water, and what look like flower petals strewn across the surface.

"Undress, or shall we help you?" Lenah says.

"I can undress myself!" I force myself to unclench my teeth. Looking down, I see I'm wearing knee-length jean shorts, and a black tank with a backward capital E emblazoned on it. My feet are bare. I'm not wearing any jewelry, a watch, nothing, but when I pull down my shorts, there's a tattoo of a hummingbird on the outside of my right thigh.

"You can give us your clothes," Juno says gently, holding out her hand. She seems friendlier than Lenah. "We will destroy them for you."

"No!" For some reason, after everything, the thought of that—of losing the last remaining things I have here from Earth—makes unbidden tears spring to my eyes. "Please. Let me keep them."

There's a pause, during which some wordless exchange passes between Lenah and Juno.

"We will have them cleaned and given back to you," Lenah says.

"Thank you."

Apparently, I'm not very modest—I'm not as bothered about being naked in front of these women as a shy girl might be. Once I've taken off the shorts and top, I unclasp my white sports bra and hand it to Juno, then step out of my plain cotton panties and place them in a neat little pile on top of the clothing she's already holding.

"Not very feminine," one of the women remarks in a loud whisper. "She has a body like that of a boy."

"It will not please King Aurus," says another.

"I can hear you," I say loudly, stepping into the tub and resisting the urge to glare at them. But their words make me realize something. If I can't prevent being taken to meet the king, I might be able to prevent his being attracted to me. Sinking down into the water with a sigh, I lean back and let it surround me, closing my eyes for a second.

Just one second, in which I pretend I'm back on Earth, in a bath, about to have some ice-cream and watch a movie.

And then that moment gets ruined.

"She has far too much body hair," someone says.

"It will be removed after her bath." That voice sounded like Lenah.

"I can *still* hear you," I say, shooting Lenah a look. She has the grace to avert her eyes.

I glance down at my naked body, which is mostly obscured by the opaque water and petals floating on the surface. I may not have shaved my legs for a while, but my pubes are neatly trimmed, and I'm nowhere near the furry gorilla they're making me out to be. How will they remove my hair? Is there some sort of alien wax? Not that it matters. I'm not going to let them do it.

Famous last words, it turns out, as just a short while later, I'm being covered in a sticky, sweet-smelling paste and having every last hair ripped out by the root, until I'm smooth and soft as silk from the neck down.

"You will have to grow this to be longer," Lenah says, reaching out to tug a damp strand of my shoulder-length blonde hair.

"I will not," I say. If I can't actually physically get away—yet—I'll be as argumentative as possible. Meanwhile, I'm constantly plotting my escape, making note of every door, every detail, everything I can which might come in handy when it's time to go. I'm also subtly gathering information via outwardly innocent questions.

If this is really happening—if I've really been abducted and transported to another freaking planet—there must be a way back. I intend to find it as soon as I can.

"King Aurus prefers long hair," a green-tinted woman says haughtily, pushing her own mane of shiny teal locks over her shoulder.

"Then it's a good thing he has all of you," I say sweetly. I wait until the gown has been pulled over my head before asking, "Are you his wives?"

"His harem," Juno says softly. "His courtesans."

"There seem to be enough of you. Enough to satisfy even the most... potent of kings." I try to hide the sarcasm from my voice. "So why does he need me?" The pale yellow gown is light as air, and so sheer, it hides almost nothing. I might as well be naked. But I'm playing along.

For now.

"As we already told you," Lenah says, "he needs an Omega. Only an Omega can give him what he truly desires."

My heart starts to thud in my chest but I force my tone to remain calm—almost bored. "Oh yeah? And what might that be?"

Juno steps forward, her expression full of reverence. Her next words stun me into silence.

"To breed."

TWO

Kim

TO BREED...

This day is just getting better and better. I trail along behind the women, those two little words running in an endless loop around my mind, making it hard to focus on anything else. The gown floats around and behind me as I walk, but I don't feel very graceful. I don't glide, for one thing. These chicks look like they're wearing skates under their dresses.

I'm still trying to remember how I got here. Where I'm from. I don't even know how old I am, for fuck's sake. I'm praying it will all come back to me, like my name did.

Whatever this weird serum is that they say they gave me, it seems like selective amnesia is a major side effect.

While I was in the bath, I asked Juno some more questions, like how I'm able to understand their language: Ulfarian. Turns out that, as well as injecting me with the serum, these mystery mages—read: assholes who've obviously never heard of consent—implanted a chip in me, which makes it possible to understand and speak all known languages of the universe. This is an insane thought but I can't deny it works—for this place, at least. When I put my fingertips up to the spot just below my left ear, I can feel the little bump where the chip is.

Luckily, it doesn't hurt. I try not to think about how it works... I do not want to fall down the mind-probe rabbit hole.

The women are chattering excitedly. Aside from the green one, none of them seem to be the least bit jealous that I'm about to become their king's latest concubine. I guess they're used to sharing.

They won't have to share him with me, though. I'm getting the fuck out of Dodge before he can even come near me. I'm scoping potential exits every step of the long, arduous way to King Aurus's chambers.

You'd think he'd have his harem closer so he's not already exhausted by the time he arrives. Or maybe he just has whichever lucky girl(s) he's chosen make the trek to see him, instead. That seems more like something an arrogant king would do.

The more of the palace I see, the more I feel like I know Aurus before I've even met him. He obviously has a gigantic ego, judging by all the mirrors. And he likes to flaunt his wealth, judging by the gaudy, gleaming furnishings. I've never seen so much gold. He apparently thinks of himself as something of a stud, because why else would he have twelve mistresses?

It looks like Ulfarri women are meek and subservient—at least to the males of their species. I don't want to know how this is achieved... Juno mentioned something about being punished if they fail to bring me to the king in time. For all their advanced tech, the Ulfarri still seem to be in the Dark Ages when it comes to women's lib. In any case, I didn't ask what that punishment would be, and Juno didn't volunteer the information.

Some things are better left unknown.

We're approaching a set of enormous double-doors, easily twenty-five feet high. They're edged in gold—like everything else in this place; it wouldn't surprise me if the concubines have gold trim around their pussies—and glide open as if pulled by invisible ropes.

The first thing I notice once we've gone through are the weapons mounted on the wall: all kinds of knives, swords, axes—there's even what looks like a crossbow. I scan them all, wondering which one I could best use. If I ever had any self-defense or martial arts training, I don't remember it.

But surely swinging a knife at someone can't be *that* hard?

The weapons are fairly high up, however, so I need to find some kind of stool or something so I can even reach one to steal it. I'm still glancing around, scanning the furniture, when I spot an enormous, gleaming figure. At the same time, I hear Lenah say,

"Your Majesty, allow me to present your new Omega. Kim."

Someone's fingers encircle my wrist, and I'm unceremoniously tugged forward.

The first thing I register is his size. I thought the women were tall... this guy is huge. He's wearing shiny golden armor so I can't tell whether he's fit or fat, but he looks to be over seven freaking feet tall, and seems almost as broad in the shoulders. He's wearing a poncy helmet, so I can't see his face, but he radiates strength.

And arrogance.

His voice, when he speaks, is low, deep, and growly. "At last. I've waited a long time for you, Omega."

"My name is *Kim*," I say, proud that my voice is calm and steady. Figure we may as well start as we mean to go on. I bow to no one.

"Kim." The way he says it sends a shiver down my spine.

I realize I don't know how to address him. Calling him *your Majesty* seems kind of pretentious when he's not my king. "There seems to have been a mistake," I continue. "I'm not an Omega. I'm a human. I would like to return to Earth now."

There's a long, long pause. The women all seem to be holding their breath, watching Aurus to see what he'll do. When he throws his huge, helmeted head back and roars with laughter, they let out little giggles of relief.

"Is something funny?" I ask. I don't like being the object of their amusement, especially not when shit's as serious as this. I've done a pretty good job of staying calm so far, considering the circumstances, but even my tether has an end. And it's approaching.

"You have been given a serum to turn you into an Omega," Aurus says, echoing what Lenah already told me. He turns to her. "Has she gone into estrus yet?"

Lenah shakes her head, her long hair rippling. "No, Majesty."

She probably calls him *your Majesty* in bed. Then I ask, "What's estrus?"

Aurus addresses his harem. "Thank you for preparing her. Now leave us. All of you," he adds, glancing around at the other servants standing silently in corners.

No, please don't leave me alone with him, I plead silently but of course, they do.

Now, Aurus and I are alone in his cavernous, pompous chambers.

"You truly are a beauty," Aurus says. "Your hair is a little short, but it will grow. And it is golden—which I like. This is the Golden Kingdom."

"No shit." I can't help it. Besides, maybe being rude will make him want to get rid of me. A girl can hope.

There's a brief pause, where he seems to be deciding how to react. Then he lets out a little chuckle, like an indulgent father. "And you have spirit. Good. We will have many strong children."

"I hate to disappoint you, but no," I tell him. "We won't."

Another brief pause. "This must all seem very strange to you. I suppose a little bad attitude is to be expected."

He's dismissing my feelings—my *genuine* feelings—and it infuriates me. "A little bad attitude? That's what you think this is?" I'm incredulous.

Aurus flaps a hand as if he were waving away a bothersome fly. "You will soon learn," he says, as if I hadn't said anything. "The other girls—and I, of course—will teach you obedience."

"The hell you will!"

"Careful." His voice has changed. It's dropped even lower, and the gruff bass now holds a warning tone. "I'm being lenient but even my patience has a limit."

"I look forward to finding it," I say, sounding way more confident than I feel.

Ignoring me, he turns away and begins to fiddle with his helmet. I suppress a smile. He's obviously not used to undoing the straps himself, but of course, he's dismissed his servants now.

After an awkward couple of seconds, he manages to get

the helmet off and lays it on a nearby table. Then he turns around.

Holy fuck, he's gorgeous! Damn, damn, damn!

His skin is a pale bronze, with dark gold tribal markings on his forehead and neck. He has a strong, striking jaw, surprisingly full lips, and the most hypnotic eyes I think I've ever seen. They're the color of burnt honey, glowing almost amber when the light hits the irises.

Pull yourself together, Kim. He might be one of the hottest males you've ever seen, but he's still holding you captive. Don't show him you're attracted.

"Come here, Omega," Aurus says, holding out an encouraging hand.

"My name is Kim." I fold my arms across my chest. "And... no." It's petulant and childish, I know, but I'm starting to feel a weird fluttering in my tummy and his direct gaze is distracting me. "I want you to let me go. Or, I'll find my own way out... I'll escape."

Aurus scoffs. "Oh, really?"

Taking a deep breath to steady my wavering nerves, I almost stagger when I smell it. Sandalwood, new leather, pine... the scent is overpowering but so good that I inhale deeply through my nose, wanting more.

That's when there's a sudden jolt of pleasure directly in my clit, immediately followed by a wet, trickling sensation between my legs. Startled, I can't prevent my gasp at the unexpected, intense stab of lust. What the hell is wrong with me?

I look to Aurus—for answers, for help, I don't know—and his eye color has changed to burnt sienna. His entire body is rigid, his face set in a leonine expression that I can only describe as feral. A faraway part of me registers that he's clenched his fists by his sides.

The twist of desire in my lower belly is joined now by a sharp pang of fear. The convivial, attractive king is gone, and in his place is a beast who's as focused on me as a lion on a gazelle.

I'm the prey.

The scent intensifies, becoming so thick it's a tangible thing, seeping into me, invading my very pores. I let out a moan as my clit thumps again. My nipples tighten beneath the gossamer gown.

What the fuck is happening to me?

Then, Aurus begins to growl...

THREE

Aurus

I CANNOT REMEMBER the last time I was so excited about something. So impatient. Ever since Khan returned from a trip with that little Omega in tow, I have coveted one for myself.

It took the magicians long enough to find a way to bring Hoo-man females here, and then there was some long, dull selection process—I don't know, I was barely paying attention when they explained it to me. I merely asked for a golden-haired one.

I am Aurus, High King of Ulfaria, and I get what I want.

Even then, when the time finally arrived and my new Omega was brought through the portal, I was forced to wait for her to be given the translation chip and the serum...

... and then wait for the serum to work...

Interminable waiting.

Strangely, though, the endless anticipation only heightened my excitement when I finally received word that she was ready to be brought to me by my harem.

I am fond of my Beta courtesans, but now I have a new plaything.

One who can bear my heirs.

I don't usually dress in my armor unless we're going to battle, but I wanted to make an impression. If she pleases me, this Omega will be my mate for life, and we will be spending a lot of time together. I wanted to give her a glimpse of her good fortune; what a splendid mate she is lucky enough to be getting.

But she did not seem very impressed. Or grateful.

She is not the Omega I was expecting.

Her hair is golden, but it barely grazes her shoulders. Her face is pretty enough, I suppose, but she is so small, I fear I would break her during the rut. And a little too slender for my liking. Narrow hips, small, pointy breasts... I prefer my females to be more curvaceous. More feminine.

Not to mention more submissive.

She is defiant, disrespectful, and demanding. Not qualities I will accept in a mate. Khan made his Omega his queen, his *majesta*, and allows her to rule at his side—at least in name. But I will keep Kim as a proper Omega. I will use her during the rut, and leave her in the pleasure house the rest of the time, with the other courtesans. She will be coddled and spoiled, and become content. One way or the other, she will learn her place.

Her reaction to me is pleasing. When I removed my helmet and she saw my face, her pupils dilated. She was unable to hide her attraction.

And now, the serum must be taking hold. She's going into estrus.

She lets out a moan as her eyes widen. She glances down, then back up at me.

Her scent hits me like an axe to the skull. Sweet. Floral. Intoxicating as honeyed wine. It travels up my body as if I were stepping into a bath, and a lust unlike any I've ever known overcomes me in an instant.

My cock is rigid, pounding. The blood is roaring in my ears. Everything around me—where I am, who I am—fades into the background until all that exists is the little peach and gold female standing a few feet away. Her scent. The look on her face.

I must have her. Now.

A growl rumbles out of me. I've never growled for an Omega before, but it's as natural as breathing. My chest vibrates with the thunderous sound, and it has an immediate effect on the Hoo-man, who lets out another stunned moan, and takes a step back.

My armor is too tight. Ulf damn my pride. Why did I try to impress my Omega? I should have worn something simple. I tear at my breastplate. I need to move freely. As I remove the golden pieces, a rich scent rolls off my skin in waves. There is no doubt about it. I am in rut.

The Omega is aroused. Her face is flushed, her lips have grown redder. I find myself attuned to every little nuance of her. The sweet, musky scent of her slick reaches my nostrils, and I suppress a groan of longing. My balls feel heavy, full, taut. A delicious, weighted desire coils in my gut like a snake.

"Come here," I manage, tugging off the last bit of my armor, leaving me only in my greaves and the tunic I wear beneath the heavy plate.

Her eyes are cloudy with lust as her gaze drops to my

chest, then lower, then back up to my face. Her protest is barely audible, but I hear it. "No."

She takes another step back. *Wrong way, little Omega.*

There are guards posted outside the door. She cannot escape me. Her resistance is fascinating. When was the last time a female—or anyone—denied me what I wanted?

Even so, a part of me wants her to want this.

To want *me*.

She turns to flee but I anticipated this, and am too quick for her. She's barely taken a single step before my arms are around her, hoisting her into the air and tugging her against my chest. Her back is to me, and she's kicking furiously.

Every time she parts her legs, another wave of her musk ratchets up my desire. But she's straining herself, and I do not want her to cause herself harm.

"Do not fight," I say, carrying her through the hidden doorway and into my private bedchambers. She weighs nothing. Her upper body is pinned against me, with my arms folded across her chest and arms, but her legs are still scissoring like she's trying to run away.

"Fuck you," she spits, wriggling with all her might.

"That's not very polite." My cock feels huge, straining towards my belly. It would be so easy to simply push it up between her legs—but I will rein in my rut and go slowly. I will make our first time good for her. To do that, I need to learn her. What she likes. What she dislikes. What makes her moan instead of curse.

We've reached my bed. Khan mentioned his Omega having a fondness for cushions, so I had dozens of them brought to me, and tried to arrange them in a manner my Omega would find pleasing.

"If I put you down, will you try to run again?" I ask.

"Yes."

Ulf, I don't think I've ever been this frustrated. Every last shred of self-control I was taught in the army is being tested to the limit by this little scrap of a female. "Very well."

Still clutching her to my chest, I lower myself until we're lying on our sides. She is no longer kicking, but she is rigid against me.

Another wave of her honeyed fragrance washes over me. I nuzzle her cheeks, some deep instinct compelling me to mark her with my own scent. A cloud of her perfume rises, mingling with my Alpha musk. It smells good. It smells right.

My canines ache to sink into the fragile junction of her shoulder and neck, to make my mark more permanent. I did not give serious thought to whether or not I would mark my Omega, gift her with the soul bond. But in this moment, it is all I want.

Patience. Let me see whether or not my Omega will please me. She must earn my mark.

There's a brief silence, while I fight my instinct to tear her gown off her shoulders and rut her into oblivion—and while she's presumably debating her chances of successfully fighting me off, and getting away.

If she has any more sense than a rock, she will soon realize that those chances are nil.

"What's with all the cushions?" she says after a time.

For a second, I'm so taken aback by the question that I stop growling. Then I realize her obvious motive for asking such a strange, insignificant thing. "Do you really believe you can distract an Alpha in rut?"

"I don't know. I don't know what that is!" Her voice is rising. It is at that moment that I scent something other than desire and defiance in her sweet musk: fear.

I was a fool not to have noticed it before. She was merely *pretending* to be brave.

How adorable.

And now, I want to comfort her. I rub my cheek over her head, scent-marking her again. My scent will soothe her. So will my purring growl.

"What's happening to me?" There is a plaintive note in her question which tugs strangely in my chest. "Why am I..." she trails off.

I squeeze her more tightly against me, my cock pressed tantalizingly against her pert little ass. She remains silent. A moment later, I command, "Finish the sentence, little Omega."

I can almost feel her inner battle. Eventually, she mutters, "Wet. I don't understand why I'm so... wet."

I could explain it to her, but I'd rather show her. So I slide one hand down, over her searing hot skin, to the apex of her thighs, cupping her over the flimsy fabric of her gown.

Then I resume growling.

She gives a whole-body shudder against me, and when I begin to move my palm slowly, rubbing her sex through the material, she lets out a moan. My cock throbs in response. I pause for a moment, and breathe. If I don't regain control, her little sighing sounds will be my undoing.

Slowly, her legs part to allow my hand better access.

I want to roar, beat my chest, pound her through the bed. Instead, I draw the hem of her gown up to expose her cunt so I can explore it.

Kim

What the fuck is happening?

A minute ago, I was over this gaudy palace. I'm supposed to be planning my escape. But now, when I try to concentrate on getting away, it's like my body has other ideas.

Flames lick along my skin, incinerating me from the inside out. Aurus's growls rumble through me, caressing my skin and rearranging my insides. The sound is as potent as a touch. Needy pressure builds in my core. That delicious, sinful scent is getting stronger, surrounding me, and the lust gripping me is unlike anything I've ever experienced before.

I've been starving; I've been so thirsty I could hardly think straight; I've been so exhausted I almost fell asleep standing up, but never have I ever needed *anything* like I need him inside me.

Am I that hard up for sex? Sure, the sight of Aurus removing his armor was one I'll replay over and over, when I'm in bed by myself. That insanely broad, smoothly muscled chest and the powerful arms he revealed bit by bit, like he was performing some unintentional, uncoordinated striptease. More of those tribal, tattoo-like markings cover every square inch of the skin he's baring. Does he have them on his cock?

I have to know.

I need him to touch me. *Now.*

And so I let the big golden asshat cup my aching sex. I push my hips up, demanding his touch. King Goldfinger needs to give me my orgasm right the fuck now.

I can always make my escape later.

Aurus

Her lower lips are plump and puffy. Soon, they will be wrapped around my cock as I rut her. Soon. I trace them gently for a little while longer, then my thumb finds that hard little nub at their apex. As I stroke it, the Omega in my arms lets out a cry and convulses, grinding her ass against my cock.

"Oh my god," she half whimpers, half whispers. She turns her head to my chest as if to hide her reaction.

"Yes." My voice deepens to a growl. A wet spray spurts into my palm. The scent of her slick rises and, for a moment, the room blurs.

I have to taste her.

My new mate just climaxed, even though she seems to be trying to hide her orgasm. I never imagined she would be so responsive to pleasure.

And she has gone limp in my arms.

I flip her onto her back, then grip her thighs just above the knees, splaying her wide open to me.

Her head lolls on the bed, her mouth half open as she gazes at me through lowered eyelids. Her hips are already rising slightly to offer her cunt up to me.

It seems I have gained her acquiescence, but having felt her gush into my hand, I want more than that.

I want her to *beg*.

FOUR

Kim

THE ORGASM HITS me like a punch to the face. Just a few little strokes over that sensitive bundle of nerves, and I'm coming so hard that my nipples hurt. My pussy spasms uncontrollably, and I swallow a moan of shame as I gush into his giant hand. I'm rigid, desperate not to show him the effect he's having on me, but I don't doubt he knows.

And I want more, god help me.

I don't fight him when he flips me onto my back, tugs my legs humiliatingly wide apart, and pushes my knees back so they're basically around my ears, exposing my newly bared, smooth pussy to his intent gaze.

I squeeze my eyes shut. I can't look at him. I don't want to see what he's doing. His scent is still thick on my tongue but I can also smell myself now, my own arousal rising, the sweet tang filling the room.

Stupid body. Stupid King Goldfinger—no, Goldprick—with his stupid huge muscles and stupid, stunningly handsome face.

I just orgasmed, hard, and I already want more.

My toes are tingling, and the tender spots on the backs of my thighs hurt where he's gripping me, pinning me down. My pussy feels splayed open. Wet. Vulnerable.

Empty.

Then the feral, growling king between my legs begins to torture me.

He's licking my pussy lips, the insides of my thighs, even around my most private hole—he's lapping everywhere like a puppy with an ice-cream cone. His broad, flat tongue laves every square inch of my pulsating, needy core—except my clit.

I'm mindless, thrashing against his iron hold, thrusting my hips in a futile attempt to direct his attention to the spot where I want—*need*—it most.

He grips me harder and begins to fuck me with his tongue, in and out, until I'm crying out with frustration. I'm so close. So damn close.

After a million years of blissful torture, he relents. His hot, wet mouth settles over that straining, aching nub, flicking it, licking it, circling it. I scream with the force of my orgasm. White spots dance behind my closed lids as my core clenches over and over, and still he's licking me, wringing every last spasm from my lit-up body.

But he's not done.

Once my apocalyptic climax has finally subsided, I expect him to stop.

He doesn't.

He keeps licking me, and my cries of ecstasy turn into squeals of discomfort as he sucks that hyper-sensitive little nub of flesh, rolling it between his lips, still holding me unerringly in place so there's nowhere to go.

No escape.

All I can do is lie there and take it, my whole body jerking, until it once more begins to feel good.

Shit. He's starting all over again.

"Please." My voice sounds like it's coming from somewhere very far away.

He laps at my pussy for a few more delicious, awful seconds, then lifts his handsome head. "Yes, little Omega?"

I hesitate. I don't even really know what I'm asking for. "Please... I need..."

"Tell me what you need," he purrs.

I shake my head. I can't ask him for what I really want. "Please stop."

"Is that true?" His fingers still.

No! My hips jerk, silently begging.

With a chuckle, he resumes what he was doing. I fist my hands at my sides to keep from grabbing his thick hair so I can rub my pussy against his face.

When a thick finger slides up inside my sopping poon, I let out a groan. "God... please!"

He ignores me, still sucking and licking my clit, and now sliding that digit in and out of my core, stroking, exploring, until he finds the spot deep inside me which makes me give an inhuman cry.

"Pleasepleaseplease..." The pleading chant reaches my ears—*my* pleading chant. My throat is raspy. How long have I been begging?

"Please, what?" This time, he doesn't even lift his head, and his words are muffled by my sizzling, sensitive flesh.

I grit my teeth. I want to tell him to stop. But I'll die if he does. "I can't..."

"You can't... what?"

I can't take it anymore, I want to say, but I refuse to give him the satisfaction. Instead, I bite my lip and start to recite times tables in my head in a vain attempt to distract myself from the sensations, the scent, the way a second thick finger joins the first, and begins to thrust. Hard.

"You're enjoying this, little Omega," he says, in between licks. "Your voice may protest but the copious slick weeping from this delicious little cunt tells me otherwise. You want this."

No! His words make me shiver, and I try again to wriggle out of his iron grip.

"I'm not going to stop. I'm going to do this for as long as it takes..."

Don't ask. Don't ask. "For as long as it takes to... what?" I hear myself say. *Damn.*

"For you to beg me."

"I *am* begging you! Please!" The last word is a frustrated, petulant squeal.

He gives a deep, indulgent chuckle. "No, little Omega. You haven't even begun to beg. I'm going to lick and lap up your sweet juices until you beg me for my cock. For me to rut you."

This time, my squeal is of disbelief. "Then you'll be doing that for a long time," I say as haughtily as I can with my knees by my ears and his chin shiny with my juices. "I'm never going to beg for your cock. Ever."

Another arrogant chuckle. "A worthy challenge. We will see."

The hand not busy rubbing my G-spot slides across my hip—his forearm is still pinning me firmly in place—and then King Goldprick does something wonderful. No... awful. Amazing. Amazingly awful.

He uses two fingers to draw up the hood of my clit, exposing me even more completely to his unerring ministrations.

"Oh fuck," I whisper, as his warm breath fans over my aching, straining little bud. "Oh god..."

"As I said," he murmurs, "there is only one way you'll get me to stop doing this." Then he licks from where his fingers are stretching my pussy, up between my lips, and over my vulnerable, sensitive clit. When his tongue delves under the hood, I lose the last shred of control and come again, screaming, almost levitating off the bed as he maintains that inexorable, rhythmic pace. Up... down... up... down...

Again, he licks me through that climax, forcing me through the hyper-sensitive stage, and back toward yet another pinnacle of pleasure... making me ride peak after peak... until I'm hoarse from screaming, and all I can do is lie there, gasping, twisting the sheets as he milks another set of contractions from me... my abused clit aching but still responding to him. He coaxes every last shred of pleasure from my shuddering flesh, and then somehow finds more.

My juices coat my ass cheeks, and still I'm gushing.

He retracts his fingers until just the tips remain inside me, using them to spread me wide until he's holding my pussy splayed open to the point of pain.

It burns so good.

His tongue is still lapping at my clit like a metronome... a relentless beat of pleasure there's no escape from. The sharp ache his fingers are now causing only magnifies how delicious his tongue feels, and as he stretches my hole wider, I can feel it trying to contract—and not being able to.

My core is raw. Empty. Desperate.

I'm on the edge of coming and have been for what feels like forever, and Aurus seems intent on keeping me right there, on the brink...

A whole new torture.

"Fuck! Please!" My voice is ragged. I'm panting from the exertion.

"Please... what?" There's a fake innocence in his tone. He's still growling, a low, resonating vibration which travels through my every nerve-ending.

"Please let me come." I close my eyes as a wave of shame floods my face.

"When I'm ready," he says, and resumes licking, apparently intent on driving me out of my mind. I don't know how much more I can take.

"Please!"

"Are you going to beg?"

"I *am* fucking begging!"

"Now, now." He nips the inside of my thigh so hard, I squeal from the pain. "You know what I want to hear."

"Fuck you!"

I'm not looking at him—I don't want to see his golden, handsome head between my obscenely spread legs—but I can hear the smug confidence in his voice. "The next time you climax, little Omega, it will be with my cock deep inside you. Where it belongs. Where *I* belong."

Without giving me a second to respond, while I'm still digesting that statement—and refusing to admit to myself how much it turned me on—he resumes that tantalizing, inescapable, rhythmic licking and sucking of that puffy, abused, and yet still needy little bud which seems to have become the focus of my entire world—and his.

We're locked in a battle of wills, and I'm losing. By the time he quickens the pace and increases the pressure just a tad, I'm incoherent with desire, and it's enough to send me over the edge.

I howl as my orgasm starts, but that turns into a scream when he immediately stops licking me where I so desperately need it. Instead, he watches, still holding my aching hole wide open, as I try to thrust my hips, chasing the pleasure he so cruelly took from me just as I finally reached it.

"I do love ruining orgasms," he says in an infuriatingly casual tone as I groan in frustration and helpless desire. "I can see that tight little cunt twitching... but so much slower than when you actually come—so close, and yet so far. As I said before, your next climax will be on my cock."

He finally removes his fingers from my hole, then, and slides up my body.

I squeeze my eyes shut again as I feel his hard, muscular chest drag over my sopping pussy. It feels good but so humiliating.

Once he's on top of me, his face hovering above mine, I hold my breath, expecting to feel his cock begin to stretch me as painfully as his fingers just have.

I want it, I realize with a mixture of astonishment and horror. I actually want to feel him inside me. I *need* to feel him inside me. Why? How? Is it the serum?

I still have my eyes closed. I can't look at him. My pussy flutters, an empty vessel desperate to be filled. My scent hangs heavy in the air, a shameful reminder of my body's betrayal.

His musk is stronger now, more potent and intoxicating than the best aftershave.

His massive, smooth chest scrapes deliciously over my taut nipples, sending more tendrils of lust straight to my groin.

Then he does something I never expected in a million years. Aurus lowers his head, and kisses me. His lips are soft on mine, absorbing my startled moan, before he forces me to yield, to accept his tongue as it plunges into my mouth and finds mine.

I can taste myself. Tangy. Musky. Faintly sweet.

He deepens the kiss, slanting his mouth more firmly across my lips and showing me with his tongue what I want him to do with his cock.

His huge, rigid length is wedged against me, pressing deliciously against my hyper-sensitive labia and clit. He's so big that I don't even know if he'd fit, but I want to find out. I want him to fill me to overflowing. I want him to fuck me into oblivion.

I've never been so turned on in my life.

"Please," I manage, the word muffled by his mouth.

He raises his head just an inch. "Yes, little Omega?"

"Please." It's a hoarse whisper. My heart is pounding. "Please fuck me."

I close my eyes so I don't have to see his reaction and hold my breath, waiting...

Waiting...

Until his tongue slides back into my mouth, licking it roughly before he rears up like an unleashed animal. Gripping my gown, he shreds it in one smooth tug, ripping it down the middle to bare my breasts, my belly, my whole body, to his hungry gaze.

"Beautiful," he says gruffly. "You are beautiful, little Omega. And I want to fuck you like I've never wanted anything before in my life." He leans over me, his eyes turning to burnt honey. "And now I will."

FIVE

Aurus

I WANT to roar with triumph. The little peach Hoo-man proved to be more stubborn than I thought... but she capitulated eventually, as I knew she would. All the years refining my skill in the bedroom has paid off. There is not much a female won't do if the right persuasion tactics are used.

I find withheld, forced, and ruined orgasms work particularly well.

My cock is leaking, and has been aching since I first caught the Omega's sweet scent, but I refuse to lose control now. This is my moment, and I intend to enjoy it.

I gaze down at the vision before me. Odd, how beautiful she suddenly seems. Those slender hips, the lean, toned thighs, the hollow sweep of belly. Her breasts are so small that they point up at the ceiling even when she's flat on her back, as she is now. Her nipples are the deep pink of a leeberry, and I roll them between my thumbs and forefingers, relishing the little mewls of pain she gives.

It is no secret that I enjoy tormenting my bed partners.

A pinch of salt makes honey that much sweeter. Some are more ready to receive pain than others, and I adore the battle of wills that ensues when I force a female to endure more than she thinks she is capable of handling, regardless of whether I'm using pleasure or pain to bend her to my will.

I always win.

This little Omega's eyes are closed, and it displeases me. I want to see the way her pupils dilate when I touch her. When I hurt her. When I make her come.

"Look at me," I order, gratified when she obeys. I twist her nipples harder, and she gasps again. The pulse in her neck is thumping so hard, I can see it. Adjusting my position, I align my rigid member, guiding my throbbing tip to the tight little hole which is weeping so freely.

Ulf, I didn't know Omegas produced so much slick. It tingles on my tongue, and sends coils of desire twisting through my gut. She's so small and I'm so well-endowed that she will be glad of the slippery assistance, however.

"Do not look away," I continue, forcing myself to control my breathing. It's been such a long wait, and I am like a starving animal about to feed. I must pace myself.

I want this to be memorable.

Her eyes are a clear green, I realize as I grip her ankles, tugging her slim legs even further apart and back. Looking down, I notice the stiff bud I've paid so much attention to peeping out from beneath its hood—swollen, shiny, straining—as if demanding more.

Not yet. First, I will claim my Omega.

With a roar and a mighty thrust, I plunge into her tight cunt, forcing myself all the way in to the hilt in one smooth move.

The Hoo-man is shuddering beneath me, and her eyes have clouded over, the lids heavy.

I realize she is climaxing.

Already.

I'm not even moving yet.

Reaching down, I give her clit a gentle pinch, and am rewarded with a guttural moan as her impossibly tight little pussy squeezes my cock rhythmically.

"I told you your next orgasm would be on my cock," I tell her, then begin to move.

Ulf help me, rutting my Omega is the most pleasurable thing I've ever experienced. Deciding I've given enough consideration to her enjoyment, I now focus on my own, plunging in and out of her with hungry abandon.

She's clamped around me like a silken vice, little mewls escaping from her parted lips as I hold her legs splayed obscenely wide and take what's mine.

I never want it to end but my climax is approaching embarrassingly quickly.

Not that it's surprising. I've been rigid for what feels like forever.

Letting go of her ankles, I lean further down and rest on my forearms, putting pressure on that sensitive spot by which all females can be tamed.

I can feel it, a hard little bump being ground against my pelvis, making her tremble beneath me. She's letting out a breathy moan with each thrust, and I increase the pace.

My balls are heavy, full, aching.

"Look at me." My voice is hoarse, thick with desire. "Look at me when I possess you."

As if with huge effort, she opens her emerald eyes, her pupils so blown, I can hardly make out the green. "Please..." she croaks.

"Again? You want to come again?" Even as I ask it, I feel the knot beginning to form around the base of my throbbing, pulsating cock. Nothing else exists but this little Omega and what rutting her feels like.

"Yes," she pants. Then, "No." She hums and thrashes her head back and forth. "I don't know."

Poor, sweet Omega. "You don't have to come," I allow. I prop myself up on my forearms, shift my weight off her. It's my turn. I begin to thrust harder still. I have to maintain some self-control, as she is a tiny, fragile little thing, but the knot has expanded fully, locking her to me, forcing me to fuck her harder in order to achieve release.

"Oh yes!" she cries, and that tips me over the edge.

With a roar, and one huge thrust that drives her deep into the mattress, I climax, my cock jerking inside her as I spurt, waves of indescribable pleasure starting in my groin and radiating out through my entire body.

Her tight cunt is fluttering around me, or maybe I'm imagining it, but that only makes me come harder as the little Omega milks every last drop of my seed from me.

Eventually, I slump down over her, still bearing most of my weight on my forearms so I don't crush her. My heart is crashing in my chest, my senses reeling, full of her scent, taste, feel.

It takes a moment before I realize she's wriggling beneath me. I rear up far enough to be able to look upon her face. "What is it?" I ask.

She bites her lower lip and looks away, hot stains of pink appearing on her cheeks.

"Tell me," I demand, "or I will make you."

She mutters something.

"Louder," I command, and she glares at me like she's

about to attack. I've had friendlier looks from enemy warriors.

"I didn't come, okay?" And she adds something in a lower voice that sounds like: *fucking asshat.*

No one has insulted me in a very long time. Certainly not to my face.

Certainly not when I'm knot-deep inside them. This is the first time I've knotted my Omega and I wanted it to be a beautiful, perfect moment.

Instead, she's glowering like she wants to bite me. And wouldn't it be delicious if she did?

I chuckle, choosing to overlook her insult. "You are not what I expected."

"Whatever."

Moving my hips a little—earning myself a gratifying moan from her—I ascertain that the knot has softened enough for me to be able to withdraw, so I do. Kneeling between her thighs, I look down at the source of her misery —and joy—watching with fascination as my seed, milky white, oozes out between the puffy, pink, slick-covered lips of her cunt.

Her clit is still swollen to twice its former size, a red little berry just aching for my touch.

"Is this what you need?" I croon, tapping just above it. "Do you need me to rub you here until you lose control?"

Her cry is like that of a wounded animal. Her eyes are squeezed tightly shut once again, the long lashes dark against her pale skin. I can feel her humiliation. I adore it.

Gathering up some of our combined juices, which are so conveniently leaking from her like a steady, unending river, I bring plenty to her distended clit and begin to rub, marveling at how hard the nub is as it leaps beneath my finger. "Do you like this, little Omega?" I ask. "Such a greedy little thing, needing yet more release when you've already come so many times that I've lost count. Does it feel good when I rub my cum over your sensitive, throbbing little button like this?"

She's trembling, her fingers twisting the sheets. She's fighting it.

"Your choice," I tell her. "You can climax now, or I can ruin you again. Bring you just over the edge and then stop... watch you writhe and pant as those wonderful sensations fade away, leaving you weirdly satisfied but without the pleasurable feeling. So which will it be?"

She shakes her head helplessly, yet another sign of her embarrassment.

I'm enjoying this so much, I'm already growing hard again. I want to test her reaction to pain, so I slap the backs of her thighs, hard, over and over, right side, left side, until the pale skin is covered with livid handprints. My marks.

Mine.

She gasps and writhes, but her scent tells a different story.

"It seems you like pain, little Omega," I continue, stroking the reddened flesh. "Something we will have to explore further. But not now." I gather more of our combined juices, shiny on my fingertips, and bring it to her engorged clit. "Now, you will endure the shame of being so helpless and exposed before me while I slather this sensitive little button with my seed until you explode from it—and *I* will decide whether you will have your pleasure, or whether I will take it from you at the last moment."

She gives a howl, and I feel her entire pussy contract beneath my fingertip, her taut, rigid nub leaping uncontrollably as she climaxes. Little spurts of our combined cum gush from her snapping hole.

"That's it," I coax, still stroking, my cock throbbing at the supremely erotic sight. "Ride it out. Just let it happen. I want to wring every last drop of this pleasure from you. And then I'm going to flip you over, and fuck this twitching little hole all over again..."

"Oh fuck," she mutters, her whole body trembling.

I give a little chuckle. "Don't fight it, little Omega," I tell her, still stroking. "You won't ever win. So you might as well surrender to me now."

She turns her head then, opens her eyes, and meets my gaze. Even though she's still trembling, even though I still have her pinned in that humiliating position, she shows spirit. She counters with a single, adorable word. "Never."

We'll just see about that.

SIX

Kim

I WAKE up without a clue where I am. It takes a moment for me to get my bearings as I blink, groggily, trying to clear my vision enough to make out my surroundings.

Cushions.

I'm surrounded by a sea of cushions.

A big purple one is wedged up half against my face, and I shove it away. I'm frustrated, full of pent-up aggression— but why? I shift, trying to pull myself upright, and the stabbing twinge goes from my groin all the way up to my chest. My abs are sore. My thighs are sore. *I* am sore.

The memories return like a bucket of ice cold water being chucked over my head.

Aurus.

The sex.

Oh, god, the sex.

I've never known anything like it. The way he kissed me, stroked me... fucked me. Just the memory is enough to make my clit pulse sharply. I begged for his cock... My face flames but so help me, if last night was repeated, I'd beg again.

Where is he? I manage to struggle into a sitting position on my second attempt, letting out a little groan of dismay as I see the state I'm in. Naked, with livid handprints still on my thighs from where he slapped me, red, raw nipples which will probably never go back down, and... dried cum. It's everywhere, a sticky white residue coating my poon, the insides of my thighs, and god knows where else.

Ugh.

I really need a shower. *And something to eat*, I add mentally as my tummy makes a desperate gurgling noise.

As if they'd heard it, three women appear from some hidden doorway—why are no doors actually obvious in this place?—and glide towards me. I recognize Juno, but not the two others who are standing a little ways behind her. While they've seen me naked before, they haven't seen me so sexed up, and stained with dried cum. I hurriedly snatch up a few of those stupid cushions in a pathetic attempt to cover myself.

"How are you feeling?" Juno inquires, a little wrinkle of concern marring her otherwise perfect forehead. If the state of me shocks her, she doesn't show it.

"Like shit," I groan. I try to run a hand through my hair but it's matted from sleep. "I'm starving. And I need a bath. Where's Aurus?"

She gives a little laugh. "I have no idea. I'm not privy to his Majesty's comings and goings. But he's always busy. He has a kingdom to run."

Ignoring the tiny twist of disappointment her words engender deep in my chest, I push my hair off my face and lift my chin. It's probably better that he's not here, anyway.

Something about him makes me lose absolute control of my faculties. I turn into a raging, desperate nympho.

Fuck my libido. Fuck Goldprick with his giant, awesome... golden prick.

"Here." Juno takes a length of what looks like silk from one of the girls behind her, and hands it to me. "A robe. If you come with us, we will get you bathed and fed."

I slip the robe on, tugging it around myself. The material is soft and a deep, verdant green. "Thank you," I say. My throat is dry. Hoarse from screaming.

I didn't know it was possible to come so hard.

"I need something to drink," I say aloud, pushing the erotic memories away. "Please." With Aurus out of the way, I can concentrate. So I'm going to bathe, eat, and escape. In that order.

"Of course. Everything is waiting for you in our chambers."

The two women behind Juno move forward to help me up, and I snap that I'm perfectly fine getting out of bed on my own. I'm not an invalid.

Humiliatingly, once my feet hit the ground and I stand up, my knees buckle, and I stagger. How long was I in bed with him for, anyway? It's like I've forgotten how to walk.

"Please let us help you," Juno says quietly. "If anything should happen to you, it is we who would pay the price."

"That's outrageous!"

Ignoring me, she turns, and I allow the other two to walk alongside me as I follow her. Each has a steadying hand on one of my elbows. I don't like being treated like a helpless maiden but these women have done nothing wrong. I'm unwilling to get them into trouble.

My robe swishes around my ankles in clinging folds. At the same time, it's almost transparent, revealing my shape instead of concealing it. I'm not liking how it feels. When I do get my strength back, I want to be able to run. To move.

After all, I'm supposed to be planning my escape.

A huge selection of weapons adorns the wall beside one of the hidden doors. All kinds of swords and long knives, some curved, some straight. I realize they're the same ones I spotted on my way in. When the harem ladies brought me to meet Goldprick. Before... I close my eyes and swallow hard, fighting off the wave of lust the memories bring. "What are those for?"

"Mostly decoration," Juno says with a little shrug. "But his Majesty is skilled in the use of all of them. He likes to always have weapons nearby, should he need to defend himself. Or us."

"Has he taught you how to use them?" I keep my tone deceptively casual. Something in me wants to run to the wall and examine the weapons further.

The woman on my right gives a little snort, and Juno shoots her a look over her shoulder. "No," she says. "Courtesans have no need to fight. That's what the Alphas are for."

"Alphas?"

She nods. "Every Alpha in Aurum is trained as a soldier."

Interesting. "Are there any female Alphas?"

"Of course not!" Juno sounds horrified.

"Why not?" I genuinely don't understand why that's such a foreign concept to them.

"Females exist to breed, to pleasure, to heal, to create... we have no business on the battlefield. Although, we are given these for our own protection. Silki?"

The woman to my right stops walking and lifts up her gown. A little jeweled dagger is strapped to her left thigh.

Small enough to hide under a garment. My fingers twitch. Maybe I can get a little dagger of my own.

We're trudging down the endlessly long, gaudy hallway I remember coming down on my way to meet Aurus. Was that yesterday? Last night? I've lost all sense of time. My circadian rhythm is messed up. "Why do you need so many soldiers?" I ask. "Are you at war?"

"Not with any of the other kings at present, no. But we are sometimes attacked by outsiders. There are those who would steal what is not theirs. Resources. Slaves. Or those who would like to take Ulfaria for themselves."

We've finally reached what I privately refer to as the *harem HQ*, where I woke up yesterday—or whenever the fuck it was. "I'd really like that drink now," I say, licking my dry lips for the umpteenth time.

Juno takes a goblet from a hovering woman and hands it to me. It's the same refreshing liquid I had last time. I gulp it down gratefully.

"Would you like to eat first, or bathe?" she asks.

My stomach chooses that moment to rumble loudly. "Eat," I say sheepishly.

"Very well. We have prepared some dishes for you over here." She leads me to a corner and waves to indicate a row of plates.

I look cautiously at the food. "Is any of it... animal?" I ask.

"Meat?"

"Yeah, that's the one." It seems some basic words have vanished from my vocabulary, along with many of my memories.

"Those three." She points.

"Thank you." I'm tempted to ask what kind of animal, but then I realize I don't really want to know. I'm too damn hungry. I move down the row, trying a mouthful of each dish. The meat ones are lightly spiced but lean, and good. There's something slimy and green which I don't even bother trying, the mere sight of it is unappetizing enough. The last dish is something creamy and sweet, with a consistency like yoghurt. It seems to be just what I'm craving, as I plunge the spoon into it again and again until the bowl is empty. Another plate holds a kind of fruit. The flesh is crisp, like an apple, and the tart flavor of it bursts over my tongue when I bite into it.

"Oh wow," I say, too hungry to care that I'm talking with my mouth full. "This is good. What is it?"

"Kiktu," one of the women offers helpfully.

"Thanks," I manage. I'll try to remember that one.

Once I've eaten my fill, I get to have a bath. This time, I'm left to wash myself, although there's always someone hovering nearby, just in case I need something.

Escaping will prove difficult. But I'll manage.

I luxuriate in the scented water, letting it soothe my strained, aching muscles, inhaling deeply to get rid of every last trace of that musky, leathery tang still lingering in my nostrils.

Aurus's scent. The one that makes me cream my panties. Over and over again.

Damnit.

Vowing to stop thinking about him, I instead focus on my main priority: escape. I will get out of here somehow. And knowledge, as they say, is power. So once I've finished my bath, patted myself dry, and slipped into yet another breezy gown—this one is a ridiculously feminine pastel pink —I seek out Juno.

"What happens now?" I ask her.

She's lounging on a pile of cushions, with her eyes

closed. Glancing around, I see the other harem members all doing the same thing—nothing. Various forms of nothing.

"Make yourself comfortable," she says. "And wait."

"Wait for what?"

She turns her head and lifts her long lashes high enough to give me some serious alien side-eye. "For his Majesty to summon you again."

"Is that all you guys do?" I'm incredulous.

She gives a little shrug. "It is a great honor to be chosen as the king's courtesan. Other Betas must work hard to feed themselves and their families. Long hours. Backbreaking labor, in some cases. Here, we are fed, clothed, and live in luxury."

"Do you get paid?" I ask.

More side-eye. "No, of course not! We have no need of remuneration. All our needs are met."

I plonk myself down on a nearby footstool, sitting cross-legged, tugging the skirt of my dress over my knees. "What's a Beta?"

There's a pause. Eventually, after apparently having decided that I'm not going to go away and stop pestering her, Juno opens her eyes fully and settles herself so she's facing me. She's still lying reclined, very feminine, a picture of seduction.

Meanwhile, I'm perched on the footstool like an eager child about to be read a story.

"Society is divided into three classes," she begins. "Alphas are the leaders. King Aurus is an Alpha, of course, as are the eight other known kings. And the soldiers."

"Are they all male?"

"Almost. I've heard stories of female Alphas, but I've never seen or met one, or met anyone else who has."

"Typical," I mutter under my breath. Then, when Juno shoots me a look. "Sorry. Please continue."

She lets out a little huff of exasperation. Pomposity seems to be an inherent trait among Ulfarri if Lenah, Juno, and Aurus are anything to go by. "Betas make up the majority of society. All of us courtesans are Betas. Betas work in all fields, from medicine to construction, teaching to artistry."

"So are there male Betas as well?"

"Yes. Of course."

Of course. I suppress an eye roll. "And... Omegas?" Since this is apparently what I am, I'm most interested to find out what exactly that means to them.

"Omegas are the rarest of all. Precious. Special. They all but died out with our parents' generation—or so we thought. Then Khan returned with Emma."

Immediately, I'm on high alert. My pulse starts to race. "Emma?"

"Khan is the Wanderer King. He travels the universe, ostensibly looking to further Ulfaria's interests, but it turns out he was really hunting for Omegas all along. And then he found one. Emma. A human, like you."

A human? Here? On Ulfaria? "Where is she?" I manage, forcing myself to sound calm.

"In Altrim," Juno tells me as if I'm stupid. "Beside her king."

Altrim. I make a mental note to remember that. At last, I have a destination in mind when I escape this place. "And why was... the Wanderer King... so keen to find Omegas?" That's the million dollar question, isn't it? What makes us so special that we have to be abducted and brought to an alien planet to be... I refuse to finish that sentence, even in my mind.

Juno gives a little sigh. "To breed. Beta/Beta pairings almost always produce Beta offspring—very rarely are Alphas born. Omegas, even more rarely. I've never heard of it happening during my lifetime. When Alphas mate with Omegas, however, they will always birth Alpha or Omega progeny."

That's it? I've been imprisoned here and thoroughly sexed up by Goldprick—just to have babies?

"What's wrong with Beta progeny?" I ask. "It seems to me they're capable of anything Alphas or Omegas are."

"Alphas are stronger. Bigger. Better warriors. They protect us from all threats."

Huh. Well, Aurus is certainly enormous. He makes human bodybuilders look like stick figures.

"Ulfarri Alphas have a reputation which precedes them all over the known universe," Juno continues my alien crash course. "They are called the Brutal Ones."

Brutal Ones. That suits. Aurus was an animal last night. Huge and delicious, gone in the grip of feral lust last night. I still bear marks from his fingers and teeth on my skin. I'd find it intensely satisfying, if I weren't so determined to be mad about it. "And the Omegas? Aside from being able to make babies?"

"They induce the rut in Alphas. They are kind. Soft. Compassionate. Feminine." She shoots me a look as she says the last word, and I stick out my chin. "But most importantly of all, we need them to breed a new generation of soldiers to defend this planet."

Hah. If Aurus thinks he's getting any kind of baby out of me... he's sorely mistaken. Not ever going to happen. "I see," I say. I ask my next question even though I'm fairly sure of the answer. "The rut?"

"I think you experienced it last night?" Juno raises an eyebrow.

Irritatingly, I feel my cheeks get hot. "Yes," I mutter, staring at the floor. "I think I did. It is like... estrus?"

"Both Alphas and Omegas are biologically hardwired to reproduce," Lenah says, appearing out of nowhere.

Those damn hidden doors. I've got to figure out where they all are, and how they're opened. "Is that so?"

"Their pheromones are designed to drive their ideal mate crazy with lust. Just the scent of a nearby match is enough to induce the rut in Alphas, and estrus in Omegas." Lenah sinks gracefully onto another pile of cushions.

"But Alphas and Betas can... mate too?" I ask. "I mean, they must be able to, if you're Betas, and Aurus..." I trail off, not really wanting to think about that too much.

"We can absolutely enjoy one another in bed," Juno says with a wink. "But that is only for pleasure. Alphas cannot impregnate Betas."

"Oh."

"What's estrus like?" This softly-spoken question from a stunning pale blue girl who's somehow materialized on my left. "And the rut? What's his Majesty like when he's in rut?"

"Annay! Do not ask such impudent questions!" Lenah scolds her. "It is none of our concern!"

I hadn't really wanted to explain, but the way Lenah treats the other girl grates on me, so I decide to respond after all. "Imagine the deepest, darkest, most all-encompassing lust you've ever experienced," I begin slowly, casting about for the best way to describe it. "Then multiply that by a dozen. Supremely pleasurable. As for Aurus—his Majesty," I correct myself hastily at a sharp glance from Lenah, "he was out of control."

Juno scoffs. "That's impossible. His Majesty is always in control. Always."

I shrug. "If you say so. It certainly didn't look like that when I was in his bed."

"The rut is known to make even the strongest of Alphas lose control," Annay says. There's a wistful tone in her quiet voice.

"Alphas, perhaps," Juno concedes. "But not King Aurus."

"So there are nine kings?" I want to change the subject. Anything to distract myself from the memory of Aurus's fingers and mouth on my clit, which is once again throbbing insistently.

"There are more than nine on Ulfaria," Lenah explains, "but there are nine known kings who combine to form the Council."

"I see." I don't see. But I don't really care. I'm more interested in the other human. Emma. How did she get here? Maybe she can tell me how I came to wake up in this alien fucking harem. I have to find her. I have so many questions. "Are they far away?"

"Some are closer than others. Some kingdoms are far away, yes. Ulfaria is large."

"Bigger than Earth?" I ask.

"That's a question for one of the magicians," Juno says reverently.

Wait, what? "Magicians?" I parrot.

"The elite Betas. The ones who practice healing and develop magic tech. The ones who created the portal to bring you here."

In other words, the ones who can get me out of here. I hope. "I see," I say again.

It's all so much to take in. My mind is racing, and I'm

getting impatient. I'm not going to get anywhere just lounging around here and looking pretty. That doesn't seem to be my forte, anyway.

"Where is King Aurus now?" I enquire. The girls seem more inclined to respond favorably if I give him the honorifics they feel he deserves.

"At training," Silki volunteers. "In the pit."

That sounds a hell of a lot more interesting than lazing around. "Can we go and watch?"

"Absolutely not!" Lenah's tone brooks no discussion.

I don't care. "I demand that you take me to him," I say as imperiously as I can manage. If they see me as some valuable Omega, surely they'll want to keep me happy?

Juno looks uncertain. "If she wishes—"

"I forbid it," Lenah interrupts her.

"I don't believe," I begin slowly, "I have to take orders from you."

There's a long, excruciating silence.

Then Juno says, "She is correct. We have been instructed to take care of her, but not command her. Only his Majesty can do that."

He only thinks he can, I add silently, then glimpse a flash of gold on Silki's thigh. Her dagger. In a fit of temper, I lunge and snatch it out of its sheath.

I don't even know how I knew to do that, but it seems I can move fast if I want to. I hold up the weapon—it feels right in my palm. Light glints off the sharp blade.

The women give a collective gasp.

"I'm not going to hurt any of you," I say, resisting the urge to roll my eyes. "But I do demand that you take me to the pit where Aurus is."

There's a long silence. An apricot-hued girl casts a terrified glance at Lenah, who purses her lips and gives an almost imperceptible shake of her head.

"No?" I say, when there aren't any volunteers. "Well, I didn't want to have to do this, but you're not leaving me any choice." Taking a huge hank of my shoulder-length hair, I slice it off with the dagger.

The Betas gasp.

"No!" Juno cries, lunging forward. "His Majesty—"

"Fuck his Majesty!" I snap, and my audience gasps again. I hack away all over my head until shiny golden locks are drifting around my bare feet. "He's not here, is he? He didn't care to stick around for the morning after, so he won't care about this, will he?" I run my hands through my short, shaggy hair, and tousle it to dust the shorn bits off my head. My skin itches from the fallen hairs. Part of me is triumphant, but part of me feels queasy with anger. "He left me to my own devices. He doesn't get a fucking say."

Is that why I'm so mad, though? Because Aurus isn't here? Because after all that crap about me being this special Omega and the rut, estrus and so on, all that pomp and ceremony, the moment he'd actually gotten his dick wet—albeit several times in a row—he decided he was done with me?

And if so... why does that upset me? Why do I care? I don't want to be his plaything, anyway.

I glare at the handful of brightly colored Ulfarri females as they gawk at me. Two have their hands over their mouths. Lenah's face has turned to stone.

"His Majesty will care," Juno says. Her voice is soft, a huge contrast to my shouted ranting. "And to prove that, I will take you to him."

"Thank you," I mutter. In a show of good faith, I set the dagger down on a nearby table, even though I really want to keep it. Interesting that I would feel right with a weapon in my hand. Silki rushes forward and grabs the dagger, holding it to her chest. She looks like I stabbed her puppy.

It isn't until Juno turns and begins to glide away, obviously expecting me to follow her, that I feel the first pang of regret. I shouldn't behave like a child, regardless of the situation. And what if Aurus decides to punish the Betas for my transgression?

Goddamnit, why is everything so complicated? I need to get out of here.

SEVEN

Aurus

THE HEAT of the training grounds is thick enough to cut with a sword. The sand burns, and so does the sweat trickling in my eyes. The oven-hot pressure and weight of my weapons is solid. Familiar. I make a point of joining my army at training every chance I can get, but today my mind is full with thoughts of a little peach and gold creature...

The way she smells...

The way she tastes...

The way her silken heat grips my cock when I rut her...

Swish! I spin and duck just in time as my opponent's blade flashes over my head, slicing through the air with the precision typical of the Aurum army. The wind from the long knife ruffles my hair.

That was close.

The suns beat down on our sweat-slicked bodies as we fight, the air shimmering in the heat. I'm focusing on close combat today, working with a long dagger in each hand, as is my opponent, a young soldier named Antradx. He is several years my junior and more lithe than I, and still I find him easy to disarm.

When I concentrate.

When I'm distracted, as now, by thoughts of the little Omega mewling as I fill her with ropes of my seed, beating Antradx is a little harder.

But only a little.

I rutted my new mate until we were both overcome with exhaustion. I had intended to rest for a while, have a bite to eat, and then rut her some more, but it seems the artificial estrus induced by the Ogsul serum is less stable than natural estrus. While the Wanderer King assured me his mate's cycle lasted a few days, as is typical for Ulfarri-born Omegas, it seems that is not the case for Kim. By the time I woke up, her estrus had faded and with it, my rut.

Her little pale face was drawn with exhaustion even in slumber, so I left her to sleep, with instructions for Lenah to take her back to the pleasure chambers if she woke up in my absence.

Meanwhile, no longer distracted by the unbearable throbbing in my cock, I headed to the training grounds for a round of combat practice.

I like to keep things casual when training, which is why I'm clothed like the others—lightweight breeches with a built-in groin protector, and supple, comfortable boots which almost feel like the wearer is barefoot. A couple of the soldiers are wearing tunics but I, like most of my fellow warriors, prefer to go topless. Ulfaria's suns bring out our markings, and I like the way the stripes and swirls glow almost copper on my skin.

Antradx's blades flash as they slice the air where my head was moments ago. I flip back, landing on my hands, then back on my feet. "Nice try," I say, grinning. "But you'll have to do better than that."

He advances once more. "I hear your Omega has arrived at last," he says, "how are you finding her?"

My reaction surprises us both. With a roar, I launch myself at him, blinded by a sudden, jealous fury, intent on cleaving his laughing head from his neck.

Just for mentioning her.

"Hey!" he cries, the panic in his voice unmistakable as he beats a hasty retreat, ducking and diving to get away from my attack. "I was just asking, your Majesty. Making conversation. Please, forgive me!"

Only when he flops onto his back in a blatant sign of submission do I stop growling and blink, the red spots slowly fading from my vision. With immense effort, I pull myself together. "Of course," I say, forcing false joviality into my tone. "I was just testing your reaction speed."

We both know that was a lie but he's too smart to call me out on it. "Of course, your Majesty," he says. "And I was out of line. My sincerest apologies."

"Accepted. You may rise."

He gets up off the ground, dusting the pink sand from his limbs, still eyeing me warily.

I lift my hand, signaling for a servant to bring me something to drink. I'm still stunned by the intensity of my rage. I have always had a jealous nature—I kept my courtesans away from male eyes for that very reason—but I've never experienced anything like what just happened.

I very nearly killed one of my soldiers just for asking a question about the Hoo-man. It wasn't even a disrespectful or covetous one. And I'm not even in rut.

But even now I can scent Kim's Omega perfume, rich

and strong as night flowers blooming under the moons. Her flavor fills my mouth. My canines ache. My cock swells.

Beside me, Antradx groans and drops his daggers. His back hunches and he swivels his head. His eyes are filled with darkness, pupils blown.

"Omega," he groans.

Can he smell Kim on my skin? The sweet fragrance of an Omega hangs over us like a cloud.

I whirl, following the line of scent. But I'm not the only one turning. The rest of the Alphas on the training grounds are baring their teeth and starting to search for the source of the maddening perfume.

"Omega," Antradx snarls, and the soldiers around us echo, "Omega."

There's an Omega here. My Omega. And my warriors want her.

I have to find Kim before it's too late.

Kim

"This isn't so bad," I scamper to catch up with Juno, who's gliding so fast, the hem of her gown is slithering over the ground like quicksilver. She's pissed at me. Not that I care. "I don't see what the big deal is."

"His Majesty wishes for you to remain in the harem." She sweeps ahead of me, nose in the air.

I jog to keep up with her pace. "He also wants me to be comfortable here. The palace is my new home, right?" I don't know if Aurus cares whether I'm comfortable, but my guess is the Betas should keep me happy.

She gives a ladylike sniff. "You should obey his Majesty in all things."

"Yeah, not gonna happen." We pass through a doorway and enter a bright hall. On one side, a long open window is open to the air. Shouts and clanging metal drift up from a courtyard below.

"Here we are." Juno stops abruptly. At the end of the hall are two huge Alpha warriors in full gold armor. I lean past her to study them. "I advise you not to run," she says, as if reading my thoughts.

The scrape and ringing of metal draws me back to the view.

"Those are the training grounds?" I point. We're high above the soldiers in a hidden gallery, behind a gauzy curtain. It's a little stuffy, but it doesn't seem as hot up here as it looks down there, with the sun beating against the sand. I approach the railing and the heat hits my face like a blast from an oven door.

"Not too close," Juno says, wringing her hands.

"I'm not going to go over. I'm not stupid," I mutter, but I step back. "What's with the curtain?"

"At times, we are allowed to watch his Majesty train, but no warrior may look upon us."

"What about those guys?" I wave at the guards. Maybe she'll send them away.

"Those are our guards. They're not allowed to touch us," she says stiffly.

They're both wearing helmets, but somehow I know both sets of Alpha eyes are fixed on me.

Maybe I can slip past them somehow...

A roaring battle cry ululates up from the training sands. I step closer to the railing. It's not like it's an open platform.

And I'm not going to dive off. I scoot closer—and when I see the tableau below, I'm so glad I did.

A row of three golden, blazing suns gleam in a pale mauve sky, turning the sandy grounds pink. Or is the sand always pink?

At the far end of the grounds writhes a mass of shining, muscled bodies. Alphas—Alphas everywhere. Big, hulking warriors, half-clothed and sleek with sweat. Spinning, weaving, attacking. Weapons of all kinds are scattered around. In the middle of the grounds is a huge platform with a giant bronze gong suspended in a golden frame.

A scent rises from the sand—not unpleasant. Salty. Spicy. Delicious man meat baking golden in the suns.

And in the middle of the sparring is the biggest, baddest, most golden boy of them all.

Everything in me focuses on *him*.

There's another roar, and a flash of weaponry. A lither warrior lunges towards the grand one. Metal glints.

I suck in a breath. *Look out!*

The huge warrior waits until the last moment and dodges, gliding past the blade like he sensed it coming. He whips around and slashes at his opponent, driving the slighter warrior back. His thrusts are so fast, everyone else looks like they're moving in slow motion.

I'm licking my lips, leaning over the railing. My breasts are suddenly swollen, aching. Heat pulses between my thighs. If I called out to the Alpha, would he hear me? Or is the stupid curtain too much in the way?

The warrior turns. It's Aurus.

Damnit. I lean back. Yes, he's sexy as hell. But he's such an asshat.

I'm not hot for him. I refuse to be.

Juno's staring at me, eyebrows raised. "Are you all right?"

"Of course." I stop wiping my brow and pretend I was trying to fix my freshly shorn hair. It's probably sticking up every which way. Oh well.

Juno harrumphs, and I half turn away to surreptitiously fan myself. All this sultry heat is making me thirsty. It's just the summer-hot suns, right? That's what's making my insides boil.

Aurus stares broodily across the arena, a sweat-soaked god of a king. Either he's unhappy, or he has resting prick-face. He looks about half a second away from shouting, "This is Sparta!" and push-kicking someone into a pit.

I raise a hand, and a strong jet of perfume washes over me: a rich, floral scent as thick as honey. I angle my head down and sniff my armpit. The smell is coming from me. It's sweet and strong, hitting my system like a shot of whiskey. My stomach does a languid flip.

Armor creaks at the end of the hall. One of the guards has pulled his helmet off. His blunt, blue face is slick. His eyes are inky black. He raises his head, and sniffs the air.

When he lowers his head, he's looking straight at me.

I take a step back, my skin crawling under the Alpha's gaze. It's like someone put a thousand fragrant flowers into the stuffy space, or baked a hundred cinnamon rolls. The scent is delicious and enticing. I straighten, willing myself to stop smelling up the place, but it's too late. I smell like an apple pie, and the Alpha guard wants to take a bite out of me.

"Kim." Juno whirls to me, eyes wide. Her lips move but I don't hear a sound. The Alpha behind her has tossed aside his helmet and is racing towards us. Towards me.

"Look out!" I shout, and push Juno aside. She stumbles

against the back wall, out of the soldier's path. He's charging like a linebacker, darkness in his eyes.

"No," Juno cries, but it's too late. The Alpha is several strides away from me, and once he grabs me, it will all be over.

My legs take off before I know what I'm doing. I sprint two, three feet *towards* the Alpha—and leap. My hand comes down on his armored shoulder at just the right moment and I fly over him, twisting in a flip.

A second, and it's over. I'm back on my feet, staring at the charging Alpha's back. His weapon is in my hand. Somehow, I snatched it from its sheath as he was rushing me. As I was flipping over his head.

Holy shit! I know Jiu Jitsu!

Beside me, Juno's frozen. Her mouth hangs open.

Armor creaks behind me. The second Alpha is sniffing the air.

I drop into a crouch, my weapon raised.

"Kim," Juno whispers. Her temples are damp. "They can scent you and they're going into rut. You must run."

"You go first," I whisper back, and she shakes her head.

With a roar, the second soldier charges. The first has stripped off his breastplate and crouched down. Now he can move more easily.

Both guards go still at the same time, sighting me, sizing me up. I scoot back from Juno to draw them away from her, until my back is braced against the railing.

There's nowhere to go.

The guards charge.

Juno shouts my name.

I grab the top of the railing and swing myself up to balance at the top. My filmy robe threatens to tangle my feet, but I jerk it up to my knees.

"Stay back," I order. The Alphas slow down but keep slinking forward. I rise, my jaw clenched as I hold up my robe, using my other arm for balance. "Don't come any closer."

Juno has her hand over her mouth.

The Alphas have noticed each other and stopped. They growl, both apparently sensing a rival.

"Juno, get away. Get help," I whisper. "Please."

She whimpers but presses against the wall, inching towards the door. At least she'll be safe.

Far below, on the training grounds, Aurus lets out a growl. It's one rich sound in a cacophony of others, but my body responds like he tripped my trigger. There's a deep, intense thump in my clit and slick gushes from my pussy, sliding down my thighs.

Shit.

The Alpha guards face me again. Their eyes are black slits. Their nostrils flare.

My feet feel unsteady on the railing. "I'll jump," I warn them. "I mean it."

The guards are too far gone into madness to listen. They lunge, arms outstretched, to grab me.

With a cry, I turn, and hurl myself into the air.

Aurus

The thick perfume is coming from above. Shouts rise from the gallery. A warning growl vibrates from my chest.

"Your Majesty!" A slim Beta servant runs up, his robes flapping around his skinny legs. Thank Ulf someone with a brain is here—my warriors are behaving like Alphas about to enter the rut. "What is happening?"

"Get them out," I snarl. "The Omega is here."

The Beta's nostrils flare. "The Omega?" he squeaks. "Where?"

I answer with an echoing growl.

Another wave of scent hits the training grounds. As one, we turn—I, and every other Alpha in the place.

There's a small, short cry and Kim appears, flying from the long balcony. Her legs and arms windmill, then somehow she grabs onto the curtain. She has a weapon in her hand, it pierces the fabric and slows her descent. With a loud rip, the curtain parts, and she grabs a hunk of it and swings down to the sand. I lurch forward, but she's already landed. Safely.

"Fuck yeah," she shouts. Now I can see she's holding some sort of knife. Her hair looks shorter, sticking out on all sides like she's been struck by lightning.

The Alphas beside me are motionless, staring.

I have to go to her, but the Beta is blocking my way. "Your Majesty—what do I do?" He wrings his hands.

"Get the Elite Forces," I snap, and shove him towards the exit. "Helmets. Shock sticks. Protect her!" I shout over my shoulder as I start to run.

The Beta scuttles off, robes flapping. He'll get the Elite Forces to clear the arena of rut-mad Alphas. But it might be too late.

I'm on the far side of the arena, opposite Kim. I dash over the raised platform, past the gong. Sand flies in my wake.

Kim's kicking at her transparent gown, trying to squirm out of the panels. The long knife flashes as she slices the fabric. Ulf, now her garment barely reaches the tops of her slender thighs.

When she's done, what's left of the gown is a gossamer, translucent tunic that conceals nothing. Her pert, pointy little tits, her leeberry nipples, her brightly colored tattoo—every inch of her is on display not just to me, but to every other Ulfdamn soldier currently in the arena with me.

And there are dozens of them.

All Alphas. Every single one's gaze is locked on her peach and gold form.

"Leave the arena," I bellow. "That's an order!"

Some Alphas break out of the spell and move to obey. But a few, the ones closest to Kim, don't seem to hear. Two or three make a break for her. The biggest of them pushes the others out of the way, and moves in for the prize.

Kim

I must have been a stunt devil in my past life, or some sort of gymnast. Or a martial arts enthusiast, or all of the above. Because I am badass. I sliced that curtain and swung on the torn sashes like fucking Tarzan.

Above me on the balcony, the two Alpha guards are scuffling. It'll probably be a while before the winner can follow me. More than enough time. I've cut off the useless parts of my clothing—not that it actually clothes or covers me—and now I can run properly.

The sand is hot under my feet. That yummy Alpha scent is calling me. I'd better run before it's too much to ignore.

I take a step, and freeze.

Dozens of Alphas are staring at me—all the half-naked soldiers who were sparring with each other a moment ago. Now, they're looking at me like the guards were—like they're wolves, and I'm a baby bunny.

And in the middle of them all is a blur of gold, bellowing something.

"Kim! Run!"

Shit. Again?

I scuttle back, my weapon raised. My back's to the arena wall. Where can I run to? Where are the damn doors?

A few yards away, a huge warrior pushes two Alphas aside and lunges for me.

Before I can think, my arm snaps back and I throw my stolen weapon like a javelin. It sails true and buries itself in the Alpha's chest. He skids to a stop, looking shocked.

No one's more shocked than I am. I just threw a weapon like a fucking warrior. I have no idea how I did it. But it definitely happened.

The Alpha grabs the blade and rips it out of his own body. Blood gushes out of the wound, but it barely seems to deter him.

I bought myself some time, but he's still going to come for me.

Sure enough, with a growl, he tosses my weapon aside and lunges for me again. Five more warriors seem to be following in his wake.

I squeak, and race away. I dart along the arena wall to the right, and cut across the sand in a zigzag pattern.

It's no use. A tall, lean Alpha is gaining on me. He's outpaced the others.

"Parkour!" I yell, and dash towards the side wall as fast as I can. My feet take over and I run up the freaking side of the arena! The Alpha slams into the wall below me and

I throw myself backwards, into an arching flip over his head.

He bellows his loss. By the time he's whirled around, I'm back on my feet again, sprinting away. I duck and weave through the rest of the pack.

Fucking badass!

But I can't do this forever.

A name catches in my throat. My breath drags though my lungs. The heat, the Alpha scent—everything in me wants to lie down and submit. But not until I find him. My Alpha.

Two other soldiers reach for me. I snatch up a weapon and slash through the gauntlet. All of these Alphas smell wrong. I need...

"Aurus!"

"Kim," he roars. "I'm coming."

Somehow, I'm back at the slashed curtain. I leap and grab handfuls of the filmy fabric, climbing desperately. A pack of Alphas are gathering in a crowd below. If I fall...

There's a flash of gold, and Aurus crashes into the Alphas. He's everywhere, his long sword swinging and beating back the soldiers. A few fight back and Aurus slices them bloody, then slams his elbow or fist into their temples. When he hits them hard in the head, their eyes roll back into their skulls and they drop, unconscious but alive.

That temple strike seems to be an Alpha soldier's Achilles heel. I file away that knowledge for later.

Aurus punches his own soldiers out, a demonic light in his eyes. He moves with beautiful, flowing, predatory grace. Brutal perfection. I've forgotten to breathe. I gulp down air before I pass out.

A huge Alpha races forward, whipping what looks like a mace towards Aurus's back.

"Look out!" I scream.

Aurus drops to the sand. The mace whistles overhead, lodging in the wall. Aurus swings his sword and skewers his opponent from behind. He whirls, and knocks three more Alphas out.

It's insane how fast he is. Maybe he's just a better fighter, or maybe he's more practiced at handling the madness that seems to have come over all these Alphas. Whatever it is, I'm glad he can best his own soldiers.

The curtain starts to tear under my weight. I scrabble for a better grip, but my arms are growing tired. "Aurus!"

He throws aside his weapon. Around him, the ground is littered with blades and fallen bodies.

"Jump," he orders, arms outstretched. "I've got you."

I push off the wall and let go. For a moment, I seem to float. Then I'm thunking into his arms. He squeezes me tightly, sniffing my hair.

"Stay here." He pushes me back, and blocks me from the rest of the arena, guarding me with his body. Drops of red are beading on his back, mingling with the sweat—but the smooth, golden skin underneath is unscathed. It's not his blood.

I hang my head. I don't know what the fuck just happened, but *damn*. He beat up his own soldiers, and even killed a couple, it seems. For me.

Further down the field, armored Alphas in full-visored helmets are grabbing the bare-headed soldiers. Those in full armor bash the rabid ones over the head and drag them away. The limp bodies leave tracks in the sand.

A few escape, and come racing towards Aurus. He sprints to meet them. The sun glints off the weapons. One by one, he takes them down, punching them unconscious instead of killing them.

Eventually, only the fully visored Alphas are left. They clear off the grounds, then line the back of the arena, spread out into a defensive pattern.

There's only one Alpha out of armor, standing on the pale pink sand in the center of the arena, near the raised platform. The biggest, baddest, cockiest one of all.

Sweat runs down the grooves of his tawny muscles. He raises his head, and roars.

My body jerks as if he's touched an intimate part of me. My head grows heavy, my lids half closing. I take a step, and my perfume hits the air.

He turns slowly. "Kim," he growls. His new leather and sandalwood scent hovers around him in a shimmering cloud, a potent punch to the senses. My bones turn liquid.

Warmth ripples through me like I've taken a shot of liquor. A wave of wanting washes through me, making me sway like a drunk. I trot a few more steps, then drop to my knees.

He prowls closer, his throbbing growls punctuating each step.

I fall forward, fisting my fingers in the sand, holding onto the ground as if the growling will blow me away otherwise. I'm a hollow, aching bundle of flesh and nerves and need. I need...

"Kim." Aurus has crouched into my line of sight, just in front of the raised platform. Behind him, at the back of the arena, are the lines of helmeted Alphas. But they don't matter. Nothing does. Nothing but this need.

Aurus's deep voice strokes down my spine. "Come to me."

I shudder, and move towards him. The arena spins around me. Too overcome to walk, I crawl, letting my spine undulate. I'm a siren, I'm a sphinx, I'm an animal whose substance is pure lust. Every movement screams seduction.

He meets me halfway, lifting me and carrying me to the platform where he sits with me in his lap. He pauses for a moment, nuzzling me. His large hands coast over my skin, checking me for marks.

"You are unhurt?"

"Mmmhmmm." I rub my face against his. My tongue licks out to taste the salt on his flesh. I'm pushing against him and licking him like a cat, and the ache in my clit pulses in time with my movements.

"Good," he murmurs.

Then he grabs me by the nape of my neck, and growls.

I convulse with a cry, climaxing in his arms. Slick pours from my center, soaking us both.

Another cry, another climax.

"You are very naughty, Omega. You need to be taught a lesson." He rubs his cheek along mine. His teeth catch my earlobe, and nip. Hard.

More mini orgasms. "Yes, yes," I chant.

He grabs at the remains of my gown. More fabric tears. I don't care. I hate this fucking dress. It's too hard to run in. I need it gone. I need his skin on mine.

"Please," I gasp. His scent billows around me, and white spots dance in my vision.

He flips me onto my hands and knees, on the platform. I arch my back and push my bottom up, presenting my sex to him.

"Aurus," I moan as he pulls my hips up. My chest is down and my ass is on display—the perfect position for him to lick up my sex. My clit throbs sharply and his tongue soothes it, sending more blissful aftershocks pulsing through my body.

His huge hands part my butt cheeks and he licks there, too. I shudder and press my front to the wooden platform, pushing my ass into his face. My pussy is an aching hollow, quivering under his tongue. He slides two fingers inside me, then a bunch more, stretching me. Another climax bursts through my belly. The pleasure fades fast—too fast.

I need his knot. Right now.

His lips and fingers leave my flesh. His giant shadow stretches over me. Hard fingers tug my short hair, drawing my head back. It hurts so good.

"I'm going to take you like this, little Omega. In my arena, in front of everyone."

Yes. Delighted shivers run up my sides. I brace my hands against the wood and offer my sex up to him. We've just fought a battle, and emerged victorious. I'm his prize.

And he is mine.

The first thrust rocks me forward. His cock spears me, burning, stretching, pushing deeper. It's beyond delicious. I writhe in his grip. Beyond the platform and the giant gong, at the back of the arena, the helmeted Alphas stand in watchful silence. We're in the middle of the arena, fucking right in front of everybody.

Oh well.

The warriors' armored forms blur into a golden haze as my eyes half close.

They don't matter. Only Aurus matters.

His giant body covers me. He plants his muscled arms on either side of my head, and thrusts hard. I explode around his cock, my body ringing with white hot sensation.

My pussy throbs, greedy for more. My wetness coats my inner thighs. Nothing exists but Aurus and the way he's thrusting his huge dick so deep inside me, he's reaching parts of me I never even knew I had.

Gone is the calculating, mocking, controlled king of last night, whose clinical precision in bed almost drove me insane with need.

In his stead is a sweaty, growling beast, who's pounding into me as if his life depends on it.

He turns my head and brushes my mouth with lips that are surprisingly gentle. His kisses capture my cries of delight. I angle my head and lick at him, needing more of his fine, firm mouth. His tongue delves deeper, muffling my cries. His huge paw reaches down to grind against my clit and it feels so good, I never want it to stop.

When his growl turns into a roar and the knot forces my pussy to stretch even wider, just as he did with his fingers, it's perfect. All my earlier climaxes were tiny nudges up to a greater height. The knot swells, pushing me higher and higher until I fall over the edge.

Clawing at the wooden platform, I scream as wave after wave of pleasure makes me contract around him, my body trying to draw him deeper, to prolong the sensation.

Aurus thrusts again, hard.

Bong! A blast of sound rings above our heads.

Another powerful thrust. *Bong!* We're caught in a world of sound, the very air reverberating around us, the waves of pleasure running through me made manifest.

Bong! Bong! Bong!

The brassy tone splashes over us in time to Aurus's thrusts. I'm coming over and over, helpless and gasping, my gaze fixed on the giant gong that shakes every time the platform hits it.

He thrusts deep—then rears up and yanks himself free of me. I cry out, shuddering in a final orgasm even as my pussy clenches around nothing. He flips me onto my back.

"Mine!" His roar mingles with the deafening sounds of

the gong. His handsome features are rigid, his teeth bared. The amber flames of his gaze are swallowed up by black lust.

Hot liquid splashes over my naked skin. I throw my head back, climaxing again.

"Yes!" I arch under the spray. "More."

Aurus is covering me with his cum, aiming a never ending stream of it over my face, my breasts, my pussy, my thighs.

"Mine," he snarls as the last splash hits my belly. "Only mine." He bares his teeth at the watching Alpha soldiers, his breathing ragged. "Death to anyone who goes near her, to any Alpha who so much as looks at her, to anyone who would steal her from me!" he roars.

There are murmurs of assent, a chorus of male voices that seem to come from very far away.

I reach down and rub his cum into my gaping pussy. My clit pulses and I arch, screaming soundlessly as I climax once more.

Aurus

My Omega is sprawled on the platform before me, her eyes glazed, her mouth half open. She brings her soaked fingers to her mouth, shuddering as she licks my cum off her skin. The sight is maddening. My knot has barely softened but I already want to fuck her again.

She seems to recover quickly from her heat but go back into it sooner than most Omegas. She has yet to have a proper estrus cycle, with nesting, and adequate recovery time in between several days of being in heat. Perhaps she needs more serum? The magicians may have miscalculated and erred, giving her a smaller dose because of her slight build.

Or perhaps she is too small and undernourished to maintain a standard estrus? I must fatten her up.

Of course, she eats with abandon. As she's proving now, with her pink tongue lapping at her cum-soaked fingers.

My cock spasms at the sight. My rage was a tight band around my chest, but it's loosening. Why was I so angry?

Kim showed up here unannounced. She went into heat and spread her perfume across the arena. The courtesans allowed her out of the harem and brought her here, the Alpha warriors beheld her half-naked form and picked up her scent. I bite my lip as I remember. The way she leapt out of the gallery and fell. She could have hurt herself. She could have broken every bone in her body. She could have been raped and torn apart by mindless Alphas in rut.

She could have died.

Ah, yes, there's my rage. Heart pounding in my chest, I glare at the row of elite soldiers guarding the arena perimeter. They snap to attention, their helmeted gazes fixed somewhere above my head. They know their king is unhappy. Everyone in the arena knows... except Kim.

If she knows, she doesn't care.

"What the heck was that? Why did so many of the warriors go for me?" she drawls. She's finished licking her hands clean and stretches her arms over her head. The movement presents her cum-slicked breasts to me. *Beautiful.*

"Your proximity... it was the rut," I tell her.

There's something different about her. Her golden hair —already too short before—is shorter still. Ragged. It sticks out in all directions, as if she's just been thoroughly fucked.

Which she has. I rutted my Omega in the middle of my arena, in front of my Elite Forces and Ulf knows who else.

I raise my head and bark at the soldiers, "Leave us."

"You don't want them to stay and watch some more?" Kim doesn't seem bothered by the thought.

I am, however.

"No. You are mine. Only mine. No one will look upon you but me."

"They sure got an eyeful this time."

I snarl, and she holds up her hands. "Easy, big guy. You're the one who let them stay. Why didn't you finish inside me?"

I grunt. I had intended it to be a sort of punishment, but the only one who seems to be suffering is me. "I wished to mark you." First, with my seed. Then, one day, with my claiming bite. If I deem her worthy.

So far, my Omega is nothing like I expected.

"You *bathed* me. Any more, and I'd be swimming in it." She licks her lips happily, and my cock throbs hard enough to send a spasm through my leg.

I grit my teeth.

"Oh, that's what I was asking about." She rolls up and twists to point at the gong. "What is that thing for?"

"That is our training gong. It summons Alphas to train, and signals the end of practice. We also ring it when one of the warriors performs an exceptional maneuver. The ringing of a gong is a great honor."

"Well, we certainly rang it a bunch. Talk about ringing my bell." She chuckles.

"I will have it removed and placed at the foot of our bed. All the palace will know when I am breeding my Omega," I tell her.

"You have the biggest ego of anyone I've ever met." She rolls her eyes.

It's too much.

I scoop her up against my chest. Her slender arms go around my neck. She presses her tiny body to me willingly, her cunt responding with another gush of slick.

"You smell so good," she purrs, her fingers running over my shoulders and chest, exploring the ridges and planes of muscle. She tucks her head into the juncture of my neck and shoulder, and licks. My cock jerks, my control growing ever harder to maintain.

"Where are we going?" she asks between lazy licks.

"To my bedroom, Omega." I pick up my pace. At this rate, I'll end up fucking her in the hall.

"Mmmm," she purrs, her body vibrating against me. She's so tiny, but powerful. Nothing like the Omega I expected.

Perhaps that is not a bad thing.

EIGHT

Kim

I ACHE EVERYWHERE, but my blood is still humming from the sex we've been having. I don't know what's causing it—the serum they injected me with, the situation in general, or how insanely attracted I am to him—but I cannot get enough of Aurus fucking me.

Rutting, he calls it.

He's lying beside me now, his huge chest rising and falling with his slow, steady breath, his umber eyelashes fanned out over his golden skin, his sensual mouth curved in a smug smile.

I'm nestled in the crook of his arm, with one of my legs thrown over his broad, naked thighs. Peeking at his crotch, I see his cock is soft, and can't help but feel a pang of disappointment even as my pussy is sore and still leaking after the last round.

I don't remember much about Earth, but somehow I know: sex with Aurus is the best I ever had. Does the serum have something to do with this? Or was I just always a nympho? I'm obviously a badass, maybe my sexual appetite was always super strong.

Yes, that's probably it. I snuggle closer to Aurus, and he puts a huge arm around me. It's heavy, dense with muscle, but it feels right. He's an asshole, but he gives good cuddles.

"You frightened me, little Omega," he murmurs.

"Yeah?"

"When I realized you were close, and going into heat..." He closes his eyes as if he can blot out the horror. It's the most vulnerable I've ever seen him. "When I saw you fall..."

"Sorry. The Alpha guards went a little nuts. I didn't want them to grab me."

"They will lose their heads." His eyes are almost black.

I wrinkle my nose. "Can you just banish them from the palace?"

He growls. "They deserve death. But very well, I will show them mercy."

"You cut down your men for me." I lay my hand on his cheek, tracing the sharp angle of his jaw.

His nostrils flare. "They would have taken you from me. No one will do so, and live. From now on, if they so much as look at you, their lives are forfeit."

I frown at him. "That's a little harsh, don't you think?"

Black flames fill his eyes. "Know this, little one: I would lay waste to my entire army for you."

Whoa. That is a declaration for the ages. "Really?"

"You are mine, Omega. All mine." His hand fists in my hair and he brings my face to his so he can nibble possessively on my lips.

It feels amazing, but part of the hope inside me dies. He doesn't see me as an equal. I'm his Omega, his possession. And that's all I'll ever be.

The thought is a cold splash of water down my lust-heated skin. Speaking of which...

"I need a bath," I tell him.

"You certainly enjoyed my seed." He smirks. "You licked at it like you couldn't get enough."

I wrinkle my nose. "Don't remind me. That was then. This is now. I'm sticky."

"Soon," he says, pressing me into his side.

"Now," I demand.

His chest vibrates with a purr, and I settle down immediately. My chest throbs in time with his rumbles. Another weird Alpha/Omega thing Juno warned me about: Alphas can purr to comfort and calm their Omega mates. The reaction is instant and strong, like being overdosed with a sedative.

"Okay, fine. A few more minutes." I yawn, suddenly content to lie in his arms. We're naked in his stark bed, the sheets and cushions long since having slid to the floor. His golden, tattooed body and my paler one look good entwined. We're sticky, sated... and it feels so right.

Or is that the serum talking? Crap.

Are all Omegas this affected by one single Alpha? Or is it just me?

Maybe I can ask Emma. I need to find her—or convince Aurus to let me speak with her. She might be able to answer some questions for me.

God, I have so many questions. And the longer I stay with Aurus, the closer to him I feel. Like there's an invisible cord forming between us, binding us.

I need to cut that cord, stat. Yes, he's amazing in bed, but he's also an arrogant, pompous asshole, and it's clear he doesn't give a shit about me beyond using me for his pleasure. He claims it's all about breeding, but a tiny part of me hopes it's more than that. A stupid part of me. There's no use believing that he wants to be with me. I'm just his pet Omega.

Screw that. I'm going to get over this obsession, and get out of here. Get home. Wherever home is. Earth—not that I remember much about my home planet. Maybe I should give up on Earth and make a new home here. I can live anywhere, as long as I'm a good ten miles away from Aurus.

Make that one hundred miles. Out of range of the stupid gong.

Regardless, I need allies. I've probably gotten Juno and the others into enough trouble with my reckless behavior earlier that they won't be willing to help me, but maybe Emma will.

We human women have to stick together, right?

I lick my lips. Aurus's taste lingers on my tongue. Why is his flavor so intoxicating? Must be an Omega thing.

I don't like this golden royal asshat, but I love his big dick. I may as well enjoy that until it's time to leave.

"Kim." His voice is a low rumble which sends a tingle up my spine. At least he occasionally uses my name now.

"Yes?"

"We need to discuss what happened earlier."

"Yeah? What about it?" There are sudden butterflies in my belly but I ignore them.

"Everything about it." He opens his sleepy honey eyes and pins me with a glare. "Your behavior was unacceptable."

I bite my lip. How should I play this? Feign innocence? Just be confident? Distract him with more sex? When I roll over to sit up, a sharp stab in my poon makes me reconsider the third option. He fucked me so hard, my pussy's bruised.

Casting him what I hope is a seductive glance, I wave

my hand to indicate my naked, cum-covered body, gratified when his pupils dilate at the sight of me. "I didn't realize my presence would have that effect on everyone. That was an accident. But did you see how badass my moves were?"

"You could have been killed."

"But I wasn't, was I? I was *amazing*. It's like I have some sort of martial arts training. Or gymnastics. Not Jiu Jitsu, I don't think, but something, anyway... amateur javelin throwing?"

"Kim!"

Oh, right. We're arguing. I sigh. "Look, if my presence is going to set the Alphas off like that, maybe I shouldn't live in the palace."

"That's not an option," he says, his tone harsh.

"Okay, then maybe I can train with you or something..."

"Absolutely not."

"Why not?" I snap. Aurus isn't the only one who can lose his temper. "What's the harm?"

"It is not proper Omega behavior."

"Well, I'm not a proper Omega!"

"That is certainly true," he mutters, and my cheeks get hot.

"Whatever." It's not like I want to be a proper Omega. Who cares what Goldprick thinks? "Maybe you should send me back and get another Omega. A better one." I ignore the painful clench of my insides.

"That is not an option," he growls, and pounces.

My thighs spread automatically for him, as if I have no command of my own body. No free will. No say. "Why not?" I gasp as the huge head of his cock nudges my sex.

"You will never leave me." He begins to inch his way inside me, and I close my eyes.

"Then expect a lot more *disasters* in the future..." I

threaten, even as a delicious ache washes through my lower half.

"Again, that is not an option. You will submit. You will obey."

"Not going to happen," I say between panting moans.

"Then you will be punished." He pushes his way fully inside me.

Somehow, the pain of it only makes the pleasure more intense. My clit gives a long, slow thump of longing. Will I ever be able to resist this golden king?

"Starting now," he continues, his tone full of menace. "You will atone for your sins."

"What sins?" I try to summon outrage, but my voice comes out breathless.

"You ignored my orders and showed up to the training grounds and made a spectacle of yourself."

"That wasn't my fault!" Well, not entirely...

"You tore up your gown and entered a field full of Alphas—while in estrus, no less!" His voice is rising. He's all the way inside me now but he's not moving.

Part of me wants him to start fucking me. Part of me wants to punch him in the face... and make him pound me into the bed. My pussy is burning even as the slick leaks from it, dripping down to coat my ass.

"You were as good as naked—that gown hid nothing. As it was designed to do. What my courtesans wear is intended for my eyes only."

"Is that what I am? A *courtesan*?" Outraged, I begin to squirm beneath him. There's another emotion there besides my anger.

Hurt.

Aurus means nothing to me. Why should I care what he sees me as?

"No, little Omega. You know you are more than that. So much more."

He begins to move slowly, almost tenderly, sliding that impossibly long, thick cock in as far as I can take him, then almost all the way out... again... and again... It feels so good that I'm struggling to concentrate.

"You are mine, Kim. But you must learn to obey. To follow. To submit."

"Fuck that." I begin to struggle again, but there's nowhere I can go. Nothing I can do. Aurus is so big and so strong—I'm trapped.

Even worse, a tiny part of me likes it.

"I meant what I said on the field," he continues, still pumping in slow, measured strokes. "I will kill any Alpha who dares to go near you. No exceptions."

I'm panting now, a weird combination of lust, fear, and anger. He adjusts the angle slightly so he's rubbing my clit with each thrust, and I can't stop the strangled moan from bursting out of me. I'm so close to coming already. Damn him.

"So you'd better not think about asking anyone for help. I am your lord and master here in Aurum. On Ulfaria. My word is law. I am the king."

How can he still talk in such a calm, collected way? I'm going out of my mind, writhing beneath him on the very precipice of a huge orgasm. I can barely think straight, let alone argue.

"Come now, Omega," he orders, and instantly, I do.

I come so hard that I see stars, my soaking wet pussy gripping him over and over. "You're a pompous asshole," I manage, then cry out when he ups the pace. "Fuck!"

"Say that again," he dares me, sliding a massive forearm

across my chest, pinning me to the bed and slamming into me, over and over and over. "Say it."

"Fuck... fuck..."

"Fuck who?" he taunts. His scent has changed slightly, the sandalwood and leather are now joined by a new, spicier note. Like campfire smoke. I breathe him in, fighting my own body's response to the sensations he's invoking in me.

"Fuck you!" It's almost a howl.

"You will submit to me," he growls.

"Fuck that." I bare my teeth. I don't care how great his dick is—I'll never be a subservient sex slave. "I don't belong to you."

"You do." He pumps his hips and I cry out as he hits my G-spot. It's so good.

Maybe when I escape, I'll carve a smooth piece of wood into the shape of his cock. My own personal Aurus dildo.

Maybe then I won't crave him like I do now.

"I do admire your spirit," he says, that infuriatingly smug smile still curving up his lush mouth. "Such a refreshing change from the meek, subservient Betas I'm used to."

I dig my nails into his biceps, fighting the next giant climax that's already building in my core.

"When I first saw you, I worried I might break you during the rut. You are, after all, just a little slip of a thing..." He leans down and nips the place where my neck meets my shoulder and I gasp at the sudden, sharp pain. It hurts so good. "But you handle me so well. And you enjoy all the things I do to you, don't you? Even when I stretch your tight little hole. You like the stretch. The burn. The pain. Your body doesn't lie. Your cunt doesn't lie."

I'm not going to come, I vow. I'm not going to give him the satisfaction. Ignoring the pleasure building in my clit, the way his cock is hitting my G-spot, I instead focus on how angry I am. How pompous and arrogant he's being. How much I hate him.

"In fact, I'm starting to think you do it on purpose," he goes on. "Taunt me, I mean. You anger me because you know how I'll react. You know I'll throw you down and rut you the way you need it. I can feel you gushing slick for me. The way your cunt clenches around me. How swollen and needy that sensitive little button grows when I play with it. You're close again now. So very, very close. But you're fighting it."

Squeezing my eyes shut, I let out a moan as he hooks my leg up higher, spreading me wider before grinding harder on my clit. I won't do it. I won't.

"You can fight all you like, little Omega. You will lose. Always. I can feel your cunt begin to flutter around my cock. It feels so good. Will you come this hard if I fuck you in the ass?"

"Fuck you," I mutter, even as my core clenches.

He groans, his dick jerks slightly, and a little thrill runs through me. He can't fight his responses to me any more than I can fight mine. So much for always being in control.

"I'm sure we'll find out," he continues, his voice a little strained. "But that's something for another day. Right now, it pleases me to fill you with my seed, to make that tight little hole overflow with it. Do you feel the knot growing?"

I do feel it—it's hard to miss the stinging, sharp ache. Especially when it so often pushes me over the edge.

Like now.

I would love to hide my orgasm from Aurus, but he can feel my pussy fluttering around him. "Good girl," he growls, before throwing his head back and climaxing with a roar.

The way his cock pulses inside me only prolongs my

own pleasure, and it's a long time before our orgasms finally subside.

He slumps over me, panting, and I lie there, trying to catch my breath, still reeling as much from the things he said as from the strength of my climax.

"Fuck me," I mutter.

He chuckles. "I just did."

"Yeah." Damn him. He gave me everything I wanted—and more. I'm losing myself to him.

"Please don't punish Juno or the others," I say. "I made them take me to the arena. They tried to stop me from cutting my hair. It's not their fault."

"It's too late," Aurus tells me. "Their punishment has already commenced."

I'm baffled. I've been with him the entire time. "When did you give that order?"

"As I was carrying you inside. I think you were a little... distracted."

I was naked, covered in spunk, and compulsively licking his neck, so maybe I did miss him giving an order or two on the way in. "What... how are you punishing them?"

He gives a little laugh. "You will find out when you return there."

"You're sending me back to the harem?"

"Of course!" He withdraws from me and I give a little gasp—even when soft, his cock is impressive. "When you're not here with me, your place is there."

"I thought..." I blurt, then pause. There's an annoying spike of pain in my heart.

"Yes?" He rolls off me and props himself up on his side, looking down at me. Incredibly, he reaches out and smoothes a strand of hair off my forehead. "Why did you cut your hair?"

"I threatened to shear more of it off if the ladies didn't bring me to the arena. It worked. You see? It's all my fault."

"Mmm, nice try. They must still be punished." He plays with the shaggy spikes. His voice goes gentle. "It's soft. Like a baby bird's down."

I'll never be able to work out how he can go from huge, feral beast to tender lover.

It doesn't matter. He's still a jerk.

The cloud of his spiced scent envelopes me, rich and drugging, like mulled wine. If I'm not careful, it'll get me high again. Not just his smell, either—the sight of his giant body, acres of firm golden muscle, curled around me as he toys obsessively with my hair. Is there anything sexier than a brutal male acting tender?

I duck my head to wipe my face. I am not drooling over him.

His purr washes over me. "Do you wish to stay by my side, little Omega?"

I look away. How do I play this? I don't want him to know how much I care. He's got enough power over me.

I try a diversion. "They told me about Khan and... Emma. He has made her his queen?"

"He has. Emma is now the queen of Altrim, albeit in name only."

"So... she has no actual power?" The Betas didn't mention that part.

Aurus gives a dismissive little wave. "Khan adores his Omega, and indulges her every little whim, but I can't imagine he'd allow her to rule alongside him, no. What does a Hoo-man know about ruling over an Ulfarian kingdom? No. She keeps him company... she will take care of the babe... she is a good little mate. Obedient."

I don't need to look at him to know he's giving me a

chiding look. He seems disappointed in the sort of Omega I am.

Good. It's not like I care.

I bite my lip and turn my face away. "So Emma doesn't live in a harem with Khan's other... courtesans?" I sound sullen but I can't help it.

"Khan doesn't have a harem." Aurus sounds dismissive. "He was gone more than he was at home—at least, that was the case before he found Emma."

"I'd like to meet her," I say, forcing myself to meet his eyes. To my astonishment, Aurus doesn't look dismissive. In fact, he's gazing down at me with a weird expression on his god-like face. It's not anger or condescension. It almost looks...

...curious. "Why? Are you homesick?"

"It's not that," I scoff.

"No?" He tilts his head, his amber eyes fixed on me. My heart booms like a gong. Being the sole object of this golden king's attention is a potent experience.

"The past is the past. I can't change it, even if I could remember it. All I have is the future—and that's enough. That's all anyone has, right?"

"So wise," he murmurs. The slight rasp in his voice makes my skin prickle with pleasure. For once, Aurus is praising someone other than himself—and it's dangerous. I could easily get addicted to him. "You are not what I expected."

Is that a bad thing? I want to ask. Instead, I say, "What I'd like to do is... get my bearings. It would help to talk to a fellow human who knows what it's like to come here, and to be made into an Omega..."

"Of course," he says. "That makes perfect sense. I should have thought of it myself. I'll make you a deal."

Immediately, I'm wary. "Go on."

"You start behaving yourself, accepting your place—stop this defiance, stop talking about escape since it's a ridiculous notion, anyway, there's nowhere for you to go—and I'll take you to meet Emma."

"Deal," I say immediately. I can't plan an escape without her help as it is, and it will be much easier to go there officially than to try and figure out a way to go meet her behind Aurus's back.

"Deal?" There's a note of disbelief in Aurus's voice. "Just like that?"

"Just like that." Part of me wants to keep negotiating. I want out of the harem. I want him to take back what he said about killing any Alpha who goes near me, and I want him to stop punishing the Betas for my actions. I want so many things, but mostly I want to be treated like an equal, not some Omega pet.

But I've just gotten him to agree to something huge, so I decide not to push things—at least, not for now.

One step at a time.

NINE

Aurus

My cock is sore and even so, the slightest whiff of Kim's intoxicating scent makes me want her again. We rutted for so long, I've lost track of time.

Still, I'm hungry now, and even though she doesn't say anything, I assume she must be feeling the same way.

On our way in, I gave the servants strict orders not to disturb us, so now I myself must lumber out of bed, find a robe, and summon something to eat.

"Where are you going?" Kim asks, rolling onto her flat belly and resting her pointed chin in her little hands. Her short pale hair is tousled, sticking up at all angles, and I resist the urge to spank her for cutting it. After all, she has just agreed to stop defying me.

We shall see whether she is able to hold up her end of the bargain.

"I'm getting us food," I tell her, locating a robe and sliding it over my shoulders. "You must be hungry."

"I guess."

She seems more excited than hungry. I didn't miss the way the light entered her eyes when I agreed to take her to Altrim to meet the other Hoo-man. Is she lonely? Perhaps I should let her spend more time with the courtesans. Maybe their good behavior will inspire her to become more submissive. So far, she's only been a bad influence on the harem.

I've already given orders for Juno and the others to be punished. At this very moment, their torment will have begun.

Good. They're only getting what they deserve. Kim should never have been allowed to leave the harem, let alone be taken to the training arena.

I speak to Feyna, the servant waiting just outside my bedchamber, ordering an array of dishes to be brought, as well as some of my special *leeberry* wine. The Beta mumbles her assent and hurries away.

After what happened in the arena, I have decided to keep my Alpha guards a good distance away from Kim at all times. They remain stationed at the outer doors and have been warned on pain of death to only approach her if absolutely necessary—in other words, if she is in danger. If they think she is merely trying to escape, their orders are to stand down, and notify me immediately. I cannot risk them chasing her. There cannot be a repeat of what happened in the training pit.

As I close the door once again, I recall the way everything went black when Kim approached me on the field. It was as if a red mist had descended over my vision. I lost all control.

I always believed my self-discipline and training would help me maintain self-control even when in rut.

I was wrong.

Even now, the memory of her entering the arena, as

good as naked, while dozens of Alphas were within scenting distance, makes me want to beat my chest and roar.

She is mine.

She will always be mine.

"So what will we do after we've eaten?" Kim asks. Her green eyes are wide and innocent. "I still want that bath. I'm so sticky."

"With my essence." I trail a fingertip down the back of her thigh, and she gives a little shudder. "I had to mark you. Show the other Alphas whom you belong to. As Khan did with Emma."

"He did?"

I nod. "At our first meeting, when he returned with her. He had her bundled in a blanket, sticky with his seed. His scent was all over her—a warning to the other kings to back the hell off."

"God. Was she really embarrassed?"

"If I recall correctly, she was more concerned about our topic of conversation—" I stop talking abruptly, realizing what I was about to mention. Kim does not need to know how we are bringing Hoo-man women to Ulfaria from Earth. How we are turning them into Omegas using the serum. Emma is still outraged by it, and is still doing her best to convince Khan to stop us. As if she has any control over such matters.

"What was your topic of conversation?"

Damn. "I do not recall," I lie. "Truth be told, she was quite overwhelmed by it all."

"I can imagine that," Kim says. Letting out a little sigh, she rolls onto her side and sits up. "Do you have anything I could wear while we eat? I feel... naked."

I chortle. "That's because you are naked, little Omega.

You do not need to hide your beautiful body from me. I have seen every inch of it."

"I know. But the servants—"

"The servants will bring the food and then leave again," I cut her off. "It is my desire that you remain naked."

"Do you always get what you want?" Her plump lower lip is jutting out now. How adorable.

"Of course. I'm a king."

She rolls her eyes. I allow it. I am beginning to enjoy her tiny acts of defiance. Not that I will tell her that.

"Tell me about your childhood." She reaches for a nearby cushion and clutches it to her chest, effectively hiding her pointed breasts and bare sex from me. "Were you a spoiled little prince?"

"I was no prince." Taking a seat beside her, I hesitate, wondering how much to say. Wondering why she even asked. Genuine interest? Or is she just making conversation? "I was a soldier. Fought my way up through the ranks, and was pronounced heir by the former king of Aurum."

"Oh. So royalty isn't hereditary here? It is on Earth. If your parents are monarchs, you become next in line. Well, first born first... and so on. In some countries, anyway. Loads of countries have done away with the monarchy altogether."

"Who rules them?" I cannot imagine such a system.

"Presidents. Prime ministers. Chancellors. Depends on the country. People who are elected. You know, voted for. The people decide."

"The people," I scoff. "How would they best know who is to rule?"

She huffs and rolls her eyes again. "Never mind. I'm not going to bother explaining democracy to someone as full of himself as you are."

"I am willing to learn," I protest. "I simply am the

greatest and the best warrior in all Ulfaria. The most suited to rule."

"Might makes right? Might isn't everything."

"Sometimes, might is necessary."

She raises a blonde eyebrow, a sly look on her face. "So if I fight you in hand to hand combat and win, I become king?"

"No." I have learned to be wary when she wears this expression. I need to stop this conversation before she gets ideas. "That bird, on your leg." I trace it gently. The brilliant colors shimmer on her pale skin. "It's beautiful. Were you born with it?" I haven't seen Emma completely naked, so I have no comparisons with other Hoo-man women. Do they all have such pictures on their skin? "We Ulfarri are born with our markings." I indicate the bare slice of my chest not covered by the robe.

She lets out a little laugh. "No, we are not born with these. It's a hummingbird. I don't know why I got it. My memories are... messed up. For instance, I know that this is a tattoo, that I went and had it done, but I don't remember where, or why. Why I chose this image."

"Did it hurt?"

"Probably. They make loads of tiny holes in your skin and fill them with ink. That's how it stays. Forever."

My cock twitches as I recall her vocal and wet responses to pain when I'm rutting her. "Did you enjoy it?"

She shrugs. "Honestly? I don't remember."

Interesting. I make a mental note to ask the magicians whether memory loss will likely be an issue for all the new Hoo-mans we bring to Ulfaria.

There's a knock on the door and then three servants enter, all bearing trays. Taking the nearest goblet, I gulp the wine down greedily, then motion for Kim to have some. "My special wine," I explain. "Try it."

She takes a sip, then scrunches up her face. "It's sour. I prefer the other stuff."

"Other stuff?"

"What they gave me at the harem."

I raise a questioning eyebrow at one of the servants.

"*Hima* juice?" she supplies, although it sounds like she's not sure.

"Bring us some," I command. Kim is already halfway through a bowl of soup. She eats the same way she fucks: greedily, and with abandon. Not ladylike at all. Her lips purse as she slurps the broth.

Ulf, I'm getting hard again. I distract myself by filling a plate with food.

"You may leave us," I tell the servants, once they have set everything down.

"Yes, your Majesty."

"This is good," Kim says, still chewing. She is nothing like the elegant, submissive courtesans I'm used to—and yet I can't take my eyes off her. Even her lack of manners is somehow alluring. Even now, as she sits cross-legged on my bed, a cushion balanced on her slim thighs to cover her nakedness, her golden hair unkempt, my cock aches with my desire to be inside her once again.

"I'm glad you like it," I say, deciding to send her back to the harem the moment we're done eating. While she clearly enjoys some forms of pain during the rut, I do not want to injure her, and if my cock is sore, I dread to think what kind of a state her cunt must be in. She needs a rest.

Ulf knows, I need a rest myself.

"It's stew—"

Kim holds up her palm to silence me. Nobody has ever

dared even *attempt* to stop me from speaking, let alone managed it. Which is why I'm so incredulous that I obey, and wait to see what she says next. "I don't want to know," she tells me, bossily. "If it's some kind of animal, I don't want to know. I just know that it's good, and it would go great with beer."

"Beer?"

She huffs. "It's brewed with... hops? I guess? Maybe you'd call it ale? I don't know. It's a golden drink with thick white froth on top. I just know I'd really like one right about now."

"I will have the magicians look into it," I say. "I'm sorry I cannot offer you one this instant."

She looks at me suspiciously, then swallows her current mouthful. "Are you actually apologizing for something?"

I clear my throat. "Of course. What makes you think I would not be sorry for something?"

"Um... I can't be the first to tell you, but you are the biggest, cockiest fucker I've ever met."

"Thank you."

"Not a compliment. You owe me a ton of apologies. You have many things to be sorry for."

"Many things to be sorry for?" I parrot, wondering what she could be referring to.

Setting down the hunk of bread she was chewing on, she begins to tick things off on her long, slender fingers as she lists them. "Kidnapping me, dropping me in a harem where I was bathed and depilated against my will—"

"Depilated?"

"They removed all my body hair."

I open my mouth but she shakes a finger. "I'm not finished. Keeping me captive, forcing me to orgasm, not letting me orgasm, pulling out and coming all over me after fucking me in front of a gong for all the kingdom to hear..."

"Is that all?"

"It's a start." Her green eyes flash. "I didn't mention the main thing: being a condescending, arrogant, golden prick—"

"Enough!" I hold up a finger of my own. "That's enough. You are perilously close to breaking our bargain." My palm itches to swat her behind.

"Our bargain?" She wrinkles her nose. "How does this break our bargain?"

"You promised to be agreeable. This is not agreeable behavior."

"You asked me, so I answered! How is that being defiant?"

"You will display a submissive attitude. And what's more, I will not apologize for claiming my rights. You enjoyed our rut. Admit it."

Her cheeks flush but she mutters, "Not all of it. Not when you wouldn't let me orgasm."

"Obey, and you will be given all the pleasure you desire." Her scent flares, and I smirk. "It is my right and privilege to keep you sated and safe."

"Safe?" She snorts. Cushions and her plate go flying as she jumps to her feet. "When did you keep me safe? You arrogant prick—"

Throwing my own plate aside, I also rise until I'm standing over her, staring her down. "Do you think I rutted you out there in the training arena for pleasure? I did it to stop dozens of Alpha soldiers from trying to claim you," I snarl, gratified when she grimaces. "Not that I owe you any explanation for any of my actions. Nor will you receive any more. I think you should return to the harem to cool off. I will summon you when I'm ready."

She's glaring up at me, her chin raised, her shoulders set stubbornly. Such spirit, even when she's completely naked, her skin still stained with my seed.

There's a long, long pause.

"Fine," she spits. "I'll go. Will I at least get something to cover myself with, or do I have to strut around your palace naked? Because I will! I'm sure the soldiers everywhere would love that!"

With a roar, I reach out and grab her throat, holding her by it but not squeezing. "Not. Another. Word! Do not try my patience any further right now, little Omega, or I will make you regret the day you were born. And tempt an Alpha soldier only if you're willing to see him die!"

Letting go, I spin around and stalk to my wardrobe, rummaging until I find one of the silk shirts I enjoyed wearing for a time. I toss it at her and she catches it deftly. Two bright spots of pink stain her high cheekbones.

As livid as I am, I still want her, Ulf help me.

"As I said," I manage eventually, watching her cover herself with my shirt in haughty silence, "I will send for you when I'm ready. Now, go. Ask Feyna to accompany you to the harem. She'll be waiting outside."

Without saying a single word, Kim gives me a long, disgusted look, then stalks over to the doors. I hear her brief exchange with Feyna, and then she's gone.

My anger is only matched by my intense longing for the peach and gold Hoo-man who seems completely unable to respect me.

Ulfdamn.

TEN

Kim

I'M so angry I can barely speak as I follow the tall, slender Feyna down the endless hallways to harem HQ.

It was all going so well! I was beginning to see glimpses of another side of Aurus—tender, empathetic, gentle—and then he had to revert right back to his pompous self. Asshat.

If only he wasn't so good in bed. That's literally the only thing he's useful for. And I hate how addicted I already am to his taste, his scent, his touch...

He'd slay an army for me, but the second I don't act like the perfect little Omega, he dismisses me from his sight. Fuck him.

I only wish it didn't hurt so much.

Feyna pauses outside the grand double doors to the harem, and a moment later, they slide open. How am I going to escape when I can't even figure out how the damn doors work? I never see the Ulfarri push any buttons, or hear them say any words.

It's all so confusing.

My poon twinges with every step and, now that I've had some food, I realize just how desperately I want a bath. I want to wash away every last trace of that jerk.

The moment I enter the main room of the harem, my arms prickle. The main area isn't the lively hub of chatter it typically is. A few Betas lounge in their usual spots, but their eyes are closed. Sweat dots their foreheads. One is curled up, her hair a bedraggled mess—definitely not typical. Another has her arms wrapped around herself, and she's biting her lip. There's a distant sound of moaning.

Oh, fuck. Aurus had ordered they all be punished.

Because of me.

Fuck.

I scan the perfumed, pretty Betas until my gaze lands on Annay. She's perched on a sumptuous chaise, gazing into space. I hurry over to her.

"Annay?"

She glances at me, then looks away again. There's a sheen of sweat on her powder blue forehead.

"Annay, please talk to me. Are you all right?"

She blows out a breath. "No, of course not. This is your fault! You did this!"

I look around. More of the Betas are approaching now, closing in on me. Some are grimacing and glassy-eyed, but I don't see any bruises or other immediate signs of abuse. "What happened?"

"We're being punished." Juno's voice floats over to me, and I look to my right to see her gliding towards us. Her face also looks shiny, and she fans herself. "But I don't think we should lay the blame entirely at your door. We should have known better." She presses her lips together before adding, "*I* should have known better."

"I did know better," Lenah chimes in, tartly. I didn't see

her sneak up behind me. "And yet I'm being punished all the same."

"I'm so sorry," I bleat. "I did ask Aur—his Majesty not to. I told him it was all my doing."

"He gave the order immediately. Hours ago," Lenah snaps. "Although I doubt you would have been able to dissuade him, regardless."

"I tried." The guilt tastes bitter, like bile in my throat. Part of me doesn't want to know, and yet I ask, "What... what were his orders, exactly?"

Silki pushes back her long hair. "He gave us milk of the korkan. It induces arousal." She shudders and beside her, another Beta lets out a little moan. "Acute, excruciating arousal."

Wait, what? "Arousal?"

"Yes. When a female is not ready to... mate... korkan milk helps encourage her desire."

Holy fuck. Aurus has given them all the Ulfarri equivalent of lady Viagra. I glance at each one in turn and, sure enough, the signs are now easy enough to spot. The fidgeting, the bright stains of color on their cheeks, the glazed eyes. "And I guess he told you all not to masturbate?"

Twelve sets of dilated pupils settle on me simultaneously. There's a pause. Then, "What?" This from Juno.

"Masturbate. You know... do it yourself. Or, hell, do it to each other."

"Do what?"

What the actual fuck? Do they really not know this? How can a dozen courtesans not know they're perfectly able to pleasure themselves?

That fucking prick. Of course Aurus would keep them in the dark regarding such matters. His arrogance is such that he'd want to be the only one to give these girls any kind of pleasure, regardless of whether or not they might want some on a night when it's not their turn. Or maybe they do know what to do, but he simply forbade it.

"I don't know about here, but on Earth, if a girl is aroused and does not have a partner to give her pleasure—or want him to—she can give it to herself. There are all kinds of ways. There are even toys specifically designed for the purpose."

"How?" Lenah's former expression of disdain has been replaced by a shy curiosity. She wipes her brow. Poor thing.

I have to fix this.

I clear my throat. "Wherever your partner touches you... you can touch, too. Replace his fingers with your own fingers. You can even find objects which are shaped like... his... you know, his member. Rod." Considering these are courtesans, they're oddly reserved when it comes to actually discussing the mechanics of sex, so I'm trying to be circumspect in my language.

"His what?" Lenah asks.

I give a little cough. "Cock." The Betas around me all shudder, and a few let out more moans. Gah, this is awful. I'm definitely going to teach them to get themselves off, if I have to show them how to do it myself. "You can even make or find an object that's the right shape—some vegetables on Earth are perfect, in fact—and use that to stimulate yourself.."

The women are all looking at me like I've just invented fire.

"Touch... myself?" Lenah says.

"Exactly." I motion for everyone to take a seat, and find a large pouf for myself to sit on so they can see me. Then I spread my legs. "You can touch anywhere you like," I announce. "Some people do it in bed, others in the bath. You can experiment. But this is what I like."

With twelve pairs of eyes fixed on me, I slide my hand down over my breast. This is not what I imagined doing this afternoon. I want a bath and a nap, but I'll be damned if Aurus is going to punish these women because of me.

He's going to fucking regret it.

"You can take it slow. Or go faster." I let my hand wander over my belly and then settle between my legs. "But I like to rub right here." I begin to rub in a slow, circular motion. "Like this," I say, hiding my wince. Even my fucking clit is bruised, it seems.

I stop. All the Betas are staring at me.

I raise my chin. "Now you try."

Lenah goes first. She tosses her head back, haughty as a queen, and spreads her legs wide. Her bold eyes skewer mine. "Like this?"

"Yup." I refuse to be intimidated. I stare back at her as she places her hand at the apex of her legs.

Her whole body jolts. Bright spots of color flare on her cheeks. Her mouth opens on a gasp, then she moans.

As one, the rest all mimic her movements. One or two let out long, lowing moans.

Crap. I forgot the most important part. "Um," I blurt, "this is usually something people do when they're alone. Not with others watching."

Most of the Betas aren't paying attention. A few writhe on their chaises, their legs scrabbling as they rub furiously. I try to avert my eyes, but the same movements are being mimicked all around the room. It's like being in a hall of mirrors.

"And it will result in a... culmination?" Silki's blushing to the roots of her hair.

"It may take a little while to work out what feels good for you, but sure, there's no reason why it shouldn't."

Cries echo around the room as several Betas find their sweet spots. Whelp, that didn't take long. I should have known they'd all be a quick study.

Except now I'm in a room full of masturbating ladies. The scent of lust on the air is a heavy perfume. My own nipples are hard, and my clit is throbbing despite its bruised state. Dammit.

But the light flush and blissed out expression on the ladies' faces is worth it.

I rise up off my pouf, feeling suddenly out of place.

The room shimmers with pleasure. Three of the ladies have grabbed chaises and are rocking on them, their mouths open and eyelids fluttering as they buck on the cushions.

One has jumped into the pool and is angling herself in front of a water spout, rocking her sex towards the jutting water.

Lenah has abandoned her poise and elegance and has both hands between her legs now. Her cries ripple around the room. "Yes, yes, yes! Oh yes!"

Fuck. I've created a monster.

I run a hand through my hair, and my fingers get caught on the matted strands. I'm sticky, and I want a bath. But I have no idea how to work the water. Maybe I can ask someone?

Juno reaches for me as I pass her. "Kim. Thank you," she gasps. "Korkan milk is so strong, and of course his Majesty has not summoned any of us since…"

"Since I arrived," I finish the sentence for her. These poor women. Maybe once I figure out how to escape, I can free them too. They deserve it.

Plus, it will fuck with Aurus.

"Um, Juno," I start to ask, but she's rolled onto all fours and is settling on a round cushion. Her eyes half close as she starts to rock.

I hide a grin. Guess I'll have to figure out how to get the water working myself.

A duo in the corner are helping each other undress. As I pass by, they give up on trying to disentangle each other from their gauzy silks. The taller of them starts stroking the other's breasts.

"Yes," the shorter one moans, throwing back her head, her copper tresses rippling. I realize it's Silki. "Like that."

My work here is done.

Kim

A few hours later, I'm lying in the sumptuous bed I was assigned in one of the booths off the main hall of the harem. There's no door, so faint light spills over the bottom of my sheets.

They don't have lamps here. They use weird, glowing orbs which seem to be suspended in the air. But I haven't had much time to check out the alien tech yet, what with everything that's been going on.

I ended up giving myself a sponge bath with the little trickle of water I was able to coax out of the tap. A few times, I almost gave up figuring out the alien plumbing and went back to talk to Juno or one of the others, but I couldn't bring myself to spoil their fun. Showing them how to take care of themselves was the least I could do. Even now, I can hear the occasional muffled gasp or cry of pleasure. A couple times, I heard ladies calling out each other's names.

God knows what that korcan milk does or how long its effects last, but it seems to be similar to what everyone around here refers to as *estrus*—i.e. what being around Aurus induces in me.

And just like that, I'm thinking of Aurus again. I roll to my side and punch the pillow. My face is heavy with exhaustion. I would love to sleep, but every time I close my eyes, I think of Aurus and our fight. My body is all knotted up.

Stupid king and his smug, gorgeous face. Every time I think he feels a fraction of something other than superiority for me, he dismisses my feelings and opinions as if they're nothing.

Somehow, knowing that he fought his way up in the ranks to be named king rather than born to it makes his behavior worse, rather than better. Had he been born a prince, spoiled and coddled and always made to believe in his own superiority, I would have been a bit more forgiving of his attitude.

Still, god knows how long he's been king for, and I've seen the way literally everyone fawns over him. I guess it's almost impossible not to develop an enormous ego when everyone treats you like some kind of god.

And he did earn his place, it seems, which I have to grudgingly respect.

Remembering what he looked like in the training arena makes my belly tighten with longing.

My pussy is still so sore from way too much sex. Even so, if a certain golden dick was to appear beside me right now, I'd let him fuck me again.

Does the Omega serum contain korcan milk?

I smush the pillow over my face. I need to think about something else. Aurus did promise to take me to see

Emma... what will I ask her? Maybe Aurus will take me to meet her soon.

Then again, he may have reconsidered after our big argument. Or he'll change his mind when he hears I showed his harem how to get around his cruel punishment. A small part of me hopes he won't find out, but it's unlikely to be kept a secret. Even if the girls keep *stumm*, there are servants—read: eyes and ears—everywhere.

And there's no mistaking they've discovered self-pleasure. Some of them have apparently been at it since I first showed them, seriously risking giving themselves an RSI...

A wild cry rings out outside my room, shrill and echoing. It goes on and on and on. It sounds like a seagull being murdered.

I press the pillow down harder over my ears. It's no use. The ache between my thighs is just growing.

My hand drifts to my throbbing clit as if it has a mind of its own, and I begin to stroke it, gently, slowly, ready to stop if it hurts.

But it feels good so I up the pace, my other hand sliding up to find my left nipple. I'm wearing yet another silky robe, and the material is smooth and feels delicious on my skin. I again ripped off the bottom section so I could move without tripping, but I'm starting to get used to these harem garments.

I kind of like the way Aurus looks at me when I wear them. Like I'm the only person on the planet. If he saw me now, with my hands between my legs, arousal flushing my chest, he'd freeze like a predator sighting its quarry. His eyes would flare a rich amber. He'd lope forward, stalking me with lupine grace. His body is chiseled and insanely muscled. He's impossibly big, and we shouldn't fit together so perfectly, but somehow we do...

Fuck, now I'm thinking about Aurus again.

Unbidden images flicker in my mind's eye: Aurus on top of me, his drugging scent making me dizzy, his hard muscles bunching as he moves, his sharp teeth nipping at my neck. There's a sudden stab in my pussy as if he's actually here now, sliding that huge cock up inside me, his growly voice murmuring delicious threats and promises as he relentlessly drives me up... and up...

It's no good. I can't do it. For some reason, even though I get frustratingly close to coming several times, I can't get over the edge.

It's like I'm under some weird, new spell where Aurus controls my pleasure even from a distance.

It's infuriating.

He's infuriating.

He's fucking ruined me.

Clenching my fists, I huff and roll onto my side, curling up, chasing sleep. But I have a feeling that even if I do finally fall asleep, the Golden King will dominate my dreams.

ELEVEN

Aurus

I'm pacing my bedchamber, wondering where the hell she is. I summoned her what feels like an age ago, and there's still no sign of the little pest.

It's still dark outside; the suns have yet to rise, and I considered waiting until daybreak before having Kim brought to me, but then I found myself too angry to sleep.

When Khan arrived with his little Omega in tow, it appeared all our prayers to Ulf were answered. It seemed like a simple enough plan: bring Hoo-man women to Ulfaria, give them serum to make up for the dearth of Ulfarri Omegas, and use them to create a new generation of Alphas and Omegas for our kingdoms.

Who could have guessed how much disruption would enter my life as a result? I didn't factor in the way the rut would cloud every moment of my existence whenever I was in it, or consider how bringing in an outsider would change so many things.

Letting out a deep sigh, I clench my fists and try to calm

down somewhat before she gets here. Showing anger never fails to make her reciprocate in kind, and as adorable as she is when she gets mad, squaring up to me—an Alpha almost twice her size—I quickly get impatient.

Such a shame we no longer have an abundance of meek, submissive Ulfarri Omegas. We tried the serum on a few Beta females, but it had no effect. And so we must resort to bringing in foreigners. If Emma is as defiant and disruptive as Kim, Khan never mentioned it.

I must ask him when we next speak.

Meanwhile, a good dose of discipline may help teach my little Hoo-man to behave and to stop disobeying my orders. Ulf knows, being patient and indulgent has not been working.

At last, the doors slide open and she shuffles in, awkwardly, looking tired. She's pale, and once again, her unruly hair is sticking out at all angles. Her light blue gown makes her eyes shimmer even more green.

I tamp down a stab of longing when her floral, musky scent reaches me.

Now is not the time to avail myself of her lithe little body. She must learn her lesson first.

"Kim." I use her name deliberately.

She stops a little way away and raises her chin, finally meeting my eyes. Even with bruised shadows under her eyes, there's a fire blazing in her emerald gaze. She doesn't say anything.

"Please, sit down." I sweep my arm, indicating a nearby stool.

She crosses her arms in front of her pert breasts, refusing to budge.

As I knew she would.

I suppress a sigh.

"I heard what you did," I say at.

More silence.

"Is it true?"

She's still glaring at me. I want to shake her.

Rising to my full, towering height, I prowl towards her until I'm standing directly opposite her, and she has to lean back to keep glowering up at me. "Is it true?" My voice is imperious.

"Is what true?" she says, once she finally realizes I'm willing to wait indefinitely for a response.

"Did you tell the other members of my harem they could pleasure themselves?"

If I hadn't been watching closely, I would have missed the way her lips curve in the briefest smirk before she pulls herself back together.

"Answer me!" This time, I say it loud enough that she flinches in surprise.

"Yes," she snaps. "Your punishment was unfair, and you know it! Besides, I had no idea they didn't know how to freaking masturbate." She shrugs. "Not how I expected to spend an afternoon. But when in Rome, do as the Romans do. And when in a harem..."

She's completely unrepentant. But even I am having a hard time holding back my grin.

One of my spies was quick to inform me of what had happened. My first response was to laugh out loud. My Omega is nothing if not devious and determined. When was the last time someone dared to thwart my will? None of my Alphas dare to challenge me, yet here I am, bested again.

By a little Hoo-man female, no less.

"Come now, Kim. You're smarter than that," I tell her, schooling my features into a stern expression. "They told you they had been given korcan milk as a punishment. You didn't stop to think that the resulting frustration might have been the punishing part?"

She looks away, and gives another shrug. "I didn't think you were still interested in their... pleasure," she mutters. "After all, you haven't summoned them since I arrived."

Her tone gives nothing away, and I consider any potential hidden meaning in that last statement. "Would you have been jealous if I had?" I ask.

"Of course not!" Her denial is too loud, too emphatic. I suppress a triumphant grin.

"I don't believe you," I say. "But it's a moot point. I have no intention of summoning any of them to my bedchamber, ever again." It's a test—a casually made statement, and careful scrutiny of her reaction.

She doesn't disappoint me. "No?" The hope in her voice is undeniable.

"No. After your little stunt, I have very different plans for them."

Red spots flare on her cheeks, and her eyes spit green flames. "If you touch one hair on their heads, I'll—"

"You'll... what?"

Her little fists are clenched by her sides. Adorable. My cock surges. "I'll fuck you up," she threatens.

My laugh bursts out of me before I can stop it. "And just how will you do that, little one?"

"I hate you." If her gaze was a dagger, I'd already be dead. "I mean it, Aurus. Don't you dare fucking kill them."

"Kill them?" I'm incredulous that she would even think such a thing. "Do you really think me that callous?"

"I don't know! If you have no more use for them... You won't kill them?"

I'm shaking my head. "Come here." I open my arms

and, to my immense surprise, Kim shoots into my embrace, burying her face in my chest. Her scent is like a punch to the gut, winding me. I fight to maintain self-control. "I have no intention of harming them," I say, stroking her soft golden hair. "I no longer desire any of them, but that is not their fault—or yours. I'm making arrangements to have them sent to the city. They will be given houses, and stipends. They can find mates, if they choose, or remain alone. It's up to them."

"Really?" She looks up at me, her eyes shining. "Promise?"

"I promise, little Omega. They served me well. Mostly," I add, when a guilty look flits across her exquisite features. "At least, until *you* arrived."

She buries her face in my chest again, but not before I catch her smirk.

I shake her gently. "Are you even sorry?"

"Sure. I'm sorry I got them into trouble."

"Would you do it again?"

Silence.

I sigh. Reaching down, I settle my finger beneath her chin and force her face up so her big, round eyes meet mine. "Since you bear the responsibility for the harem's defiance, it's only fair that you be the one to be punished."

"Whatever." But I don't miss the flare of arousal in her scent.

"You need to learn your place," I growl, and am gratified to hear her gasp as my chest rumbles against her. "You have certainly earned a host of punishments. If you insist on continued disobedience, I'll have to get creative."

Now she's shifting in my embrace. "Fine. Get it over with."

"We had an agreement," I go on, "and you broke it within moments of leaving my bedchamber."

There's a pause. "Does that mean we're not going to go see Emma?" she asks in a small voice.

I had considered that, and decided that we should still go. I want to find out whether Khan has any more knowledge about Hoo-mans, the serum, and so on. He and I have an uneasy acquaintance but unfortunately, he is currently the only Ulfarri king who also has a Hoo-man Omega. "No," I say, "we're still going to see them. Later."

"Okay. Good," she mutters.

"Take off your gown."

The change in her expression is instantaneous. Her pupils dilate, and she leans back a bit. "What?"

"You heard me. It's time for your punishment." I take a step back from her. She grabs the hem of her gown and hesitates.

I give an imperial nod. "Go on..."

Her cheeks flame but her expression turns obstinate.

"Unless you'd rather I punish the Betas in your place..."

"No!" She rips off her gown, stripping it from her arms so violently, the delicate fabric tears. It flutters to the ground, and she kicks it. "Don't touch them."

My breath catches at the sight of her slight form. Naked, she has her hands fisted at her sides again, her whole body quivering with defiance. "I have no desire to touch them." My voice thickens, along with my cock.

"Let's get this over with then."

"Eager, are you?"

"I... no. Fuck you."

My voice turns hard. "You promised: no more defiance."

"Fuck," she mutters. "Fine. I'm naked now. What's next?" Her submission is more contrary than ever.

"I'll punish you the way most Ulfarri males punish their naughty mates."

Her pupils dilate. "Which is?"

"You will find out." Taking her upper arm, I lead her over to the bed. "Bend over, and place your hands on the mattress," I say.

"Oh god." Her voice is a mere whisper, but she does as I command.

"I hear some females find this quite pleasurable," I say casually, taking my place beside her. "Then again, I suppose it depends on how hard they are spanked. I will take into consideration that this is the first time I have to punish you. If there is a second time, I can assure you it will be a lot worse."

She doesn't say anything. She's a vision of perfection with her tight little ass, slim thighs, and narrow hips. My hands are so big and her buttocks so small that this will likely hurt her more than it might a female with a plumper behind.

We shall see.

The little pouch of her sex is framed so perfectly in this position, I resolve to get the discipline over with quickly so I can rut her again. My cock has been throbbing in my breeches ever since she entered the room in a cloud of that floral scent. She will not be experiencing any release this time, however.

After all, this is a punishment.

My hand comes down on her ass with an almighty wallop, and she flinches gratifyingly. "Ow!" she says, sounding startled.

"Hush, I'm not even hitting you that hard," I lie, then begin to spank her in earnest.

Over and over again, my broad palm connects with her

taut, smooth ass and upper thighs, painting the formerly pale skin increasingly darker shades of pink—until the entire area is swollen and hot to the touch.

Kim takes it stoically, not moving, not lifting her hands from the bed, or stamping her feet. The only signs that she even feels what I'm doing are the way she flinches, and her ragged breathing—with the occasional gasp when I strike the backs of her thighs.

My palm is stinging when I've finally decided that I'm done, and my cock is so rigid, it hurts.

Placing my other hand on her lower back to signal that she must remain in place, I slide my fingers to that pink, puffy little pouch between her asscheeks and find the hard little button between her nether lips.

Ulf, she's soaking wet. The moment my fingertip parts her sex, a gush of slick dribbles out.

Kim lets out a garbled moan which goes straight to my groin.

She enjoys pain. Could it be that she enjoyed this?

I stroke her for a few long, leisurely moments, keeping my voice low. "Good little Omega," I say, "you took your punishment so well. All is forgiven now. But beware: if you disobey me again, I will take a leather strap to this little butt of yours."

She gasps, and I dip inside to gather more of her slick before bringing it back to the center of her pleasure, rubbing slow circles around her swollen clit the way experience has taught me brings her right to the edge—but not over it.

"It seems you enjoyed it, though, did you not? You're so very wet... and so very close..."

Her thighs are trembling, and for a second, I debate whether to let her climax after all.

No. She has not earned it. I remove my fingers from her

sex and free my cock from my breeches. "You will not come tonight," I tell her casually, guiding the head of my shaft to her dripping pussy. "I will rut you, and you will not climax. That's the other part of your punishment." I drive myself up inside her in one long, smooth thrust with such force, she tips forward and almost loses her balance. Gripping her hips, I begin to move. "And don't think you can sneak one past me, either. I will not hesitate to pull out."

"Please," she whispers—but I did not miss the way she clenched around me at my words.

"You brought this on yourself," I tell her, yanking her up and onto me, over and over again, rutting her to make myself feel good, with no concern for her pleasure. "I never reward disobedience. You would do well to learn that lesson sooner rather than later."

I keep my promise, pulling out every time her pussy gives that telltale flutter which lets me know her culmination is approaching, and waiting a few good moments before once more thrusting deep inside her. I deny her three climaxes, fucking her hard and fast between each, before the knot begins to form.

Aware that the additional burn and stretch of the knot usually tips her over the edge, I withdraw and rub myself to completion, painting her mottled, hot pink ass with milky white stripes of my seed.

Her desperate, pleading cries only inflame me more, and I come so hard and for so long, the pleasure burns like a brand at the base of my spine.

Eventually, my spasms subside and I draw her up gently, turning her to pull her into my arms.

She's still quivering, her body tight with tension. "It's all over," I croon into her silky hair. "You are forgiven."

"I hate you," she mutters.

"I know. So you keep saying." I keep my voice even, never betraying the pang in my heart. Why should I care if she hates me? She clings to me, and takes my knot. That is all that should matter. But for some reason, at this moment, it's not enough. "Are you upset because I hurt you?"

"You didn't hurt me. None of it hurt." Such an attitude. Even now, when she's been thoroughly spanked and sexually frustrated. She's lying. My hand is still sore. Her butt is hot to the touch, and her pussy is dripping.

"Then why are you upset?"

She doesn't reply, but clutches me harder, her fingertips digging into my skin.

I hold her tight, wondering why there's a strange pulling sensation deep in my chest.

Legend tells of a special bond between Alphas and Omegas. The soul bond. After the claiming bite, a connection forms between an Alpha and the Omega he's chosen as his life mate.

I never intended to bond with my Omega. It's not necessary for breeding. But I wonder, what would it be like? To share myself with another, allow them into my mind... How would it feel to never be alone again?

Even though the soul bond is not necessary, it is something to consider. I want to possess every part of Kim, feel her thoughts and feelings. And she would feel mine. Perhaps it would allow her to acquiesce more fully to my needs.

And I could sense what she's feeling. I am itching to know her thoughts. To decipher the shadow of her moods behind the expressions that pass over her pixie-like face.

Maybe with the soul bond, I wouldn't have to wonder what she's thinking. I've tasted her essence, I've knotted her thoroughly. She is closer to me than any other, but I want her closer still.

"Do you think you've learned your lesson?" I ask.

More silence.

"No matter. Time will tell. In the meantime, let's try and get some sleep." A glance at the crack in the curtains tells me the suns have risen, and yet Kim and I have been up almost all night. We both need more rest.

I manage to get us settled in bed without letting go of my little Omega, and despite her sullen silence, despite her obvious frustration and anger with me, she clutches me close. Her breathing slows until she falls asleep in my arms.

Where she belongs.

TWELVE

Kim

AURUS WOKE ME WITH AN ORGASM. With his big, golden head between my thighs and his broad, flat tongue lapping at my clit, I was coming before I was even completely awake.

After the denial and my punishment earlier, the release was almost painful in itself, and he made it last a long, long time, only relenting and plunging himself into me when I was begging incoherently.

I love and hate how he reduces me to that: a helpless, pleading mess.

Still, I was thrilled to be forgiven, beyond relieved that the harem girls were going to be sent away and given nice houses, and a little ashamed at how much I enjoyed the way Aurus spanked me earlier. I've already resolved never to earn myself another punishment again—the way my body reacts to him is nothing short of humiliating.

None of that seems to matter now, since we're heading

over to Altrim to see Khan and Emma. I'm finally going to meet her—a fellow human, someone else who's been given this weird serum, and can relate to what I'm going through.

I can't wait.

Aurus has this air of indulgence about him, like a benevolent king granting his poorest subject some kind of favor. Normally, it would infuriate me but I'm too excited to care.

"How long has Emma been here?" We're flying in some kind of hovercraft-plane hybrid, and I have no idea how long it will take to reach Khan's kingdom, but the view from the windows is so interesting, I don't think I'll care if it takes a little while.

"Not too long," Aurus says, "but long enough that she is now with child."

"Wow, really?" I digest this information. So humans can get pregnant by Ulfarri. What will the baby be like? How many traits will it share with its mother, how many with its father?

Poor Emma. Aurus is possessive enough as it is, he'd be ultra controlling if I got knocked up.

He can keep dreaming. I don't think the magicians, as they're referred to around here, found my IUD when they brought me here and chipped me. Thank fuck.

"Do you know if Emma is happy?" I ask.

"Khan dotes on her." Aurus sounds dismissive. Interesting. Maybe there's some weird kind of rivalry between him and the other kings.

A pretty Beta glides up and offers us both drinks. I take a big slug of the spicy juice, and smile my thanks. Aurus simply takes his goblet, barely sparing her a second glance.

Such a pompous ass.

I wish he wasn't so damn attractive, or good in bed. It would make hating him a whole lot easier.

"We've arrived," Aurus says, and I feel the vehicle shudder to a halt. He stands and strides to the door, with me following behind him like a loyal little puppy. Then he steps onto a platform which seems to be hovering in the air. It's like a magic carpet made of glass. I hesitate. It's a long, long drop if I stumble.

"Is this thing safe?" I ask. I might be a badass, but this is a little weird.

"The best way to travel shorter distances," Aurus says, reaching out and helping me onto the contraption. It feels sturdier than it looks, but I wish it wasn't transparent. I don't need to see just how far I would plunge to my immediate death if I fall.

"How do you steer it?" I ask.

"With this." Aurus taps a joystick before seizing it and pulling it towards him. I almost lose my footing as the platform zooms off.

"Jesus!"

"Hold on, little Omega."

I would, but there's nothing to hold on to. Except him. And I refuse to touch him right now. Let him beg me to touch him for once.

I curse under my breath as we pick up speed. The air is a little thin, but the mountains in the distance are stunning, rising to greet the clouds. The platform zooms low over the smooth blue-black surface of a lake, and goosebumps rise on my arms. Altrim is beautiful, with deep valleys filled with mirror-smooth lakes. The homes are built right into the mountains—sleek, dark, modern designs that are somehow perched on top of waterfalls.

By the time we pull up to what I assume is Khan's palace—a huge mountain face dotted with glass and stone structures layered between waterfalls—I'm in love with the zooming platform. When I get out of the palace, I'm definitely figuring out how to get one of these. So much more fun than a car.

"King Aurus." An insanely tall, broad Ulfarri with long, midnight blue hair and intense eyes strides towards us. Goddam, they grow these Ulfarri Alphas big. Although Aurus's muscles have more bulk, this one is no slouch. His yummy lean muscles flex as he stops and assumes a commanding pose.

This has got to be Khan. But where's Emma? There's no sign of another woman on the stone slab we've landed on. No one peeking around the door.

Khan looks down at me from his impressive height. "And this must be Kim."

"My Omega," Aurus says, gripping my bicep and drawing me right up against him before wrapping a possessive arm around me. "Indeed. Is she not exquisite?"

"Tiny," Khan agrees, as if that were the same thing. I suppress a sigh.

"Nice to meet you... er..." I cast about for the right honorific, then figure I can use the universal one for royalty, "Your Grace."

"Likewise." As imposing as Khan looks, his expression is warm and friendly. Not threatening.

"Is Emma here?" I blurt out before I can stop myself.

"She's in her painting studio," Khan says, "I will have Calla take you to her." He beckons a hooded servant over and turns to Aurus. "I thought we might speak alone. Unless you had other plans?'

He's careful not to look at me for anything longer than the briefest cursory glance. Is that protocol, or is it because of the huge golden beast beside me glowering at him with barely disguised jealousy all over his handsome features?

"I take it Emma is alone in her studio?" Aurus asks.

"Of course. Aside from the occasional Beta attendant to bring her refreshments, should she request them."

"Female attendant, I presume?" Aurus continues.

God. The guy needs to work on his obvious jealousy issues. "Calla, please take me to see Emma," I cut in, using the imperious tone I learned while in the harem.

Aurus stiffens. I try to push away from him but he holds me still. Khan blinks at me. The servant is frozen between us. Slowly, she—Calla is a she—lowers her hood and gives her king a questioning look. He, in turn, raises a brow at Aurus.

"Very well," Aurus says, sounding amused. He slowly releases me, pressing a brief kiss to my head. "Behave yourself," he murmurs under his breath, and I have to bite my tongue. I want to see Emma, and I'm aware that he could take me back to Aurum at any moment. I need to behave.

"Of course," I say sweetly, before following Calla onto another platform transport thing.

The palace is truly beautiful. Where Aurus's is all pomp and gaudy, gilded columns, almost more gold than you can stand to look at, Khan's is built into the side of the mountain. The giant rock platforms lead to towering rooms of black obsidian, closed off from the elements by several stories' worth of glass. The structures are built in sleek architectural lines, very modern but close to nature. Streams flow in grooves down the sides of the rock platforms, and turn into waterfalls crashing onto the rock platforms below. The air is cool from the mist. Calla and I zoom around a waterfall to an unassuming entrance hewn into the rock. The platform pulls to a halt, and Calla offers me her hand to help me off.

For a second, I feel bad. If Emma's painting, I don't

want to disturb her. Then again, this may be my only chance to talk to her.

Calla raps on the door, then glides inside once it opens. She walks the same way the Beta women in Aurum do, like she's wearing skates under her gown. "Majesta," she says loudly. "You have a visitor."

I barely have a moment to take in the gorgeous, moving paintings lined around the walls before an astonishingly pretty blonde appears from behind a vast canvas and comes toward us. Her pale skin and human features are almost startling after being around only aliens for so long. "Thank you, Calla," she says, pushing a stray strand of hair off her forehead. "You may leave us."

"Would you like any refreshments?" Calla asks, as if unwilling to let us be alone.

Emma waves at a nearby table holding a tray and goblets. "Already taken care of." She gives Calla a sweet smile. "You may go."

"Very well." The pale green woman turns and glides back through the door we just came through.

"She's nice, but very nosy," Emma says with an impish grin. "You must be Kim." She has a slight British accent, but it's still so good to hear English again, just pure, unadulterated English without the in-brain translation, that I almost feel dizzy with joy.

"I am," I tell her. "It's so good to meet you. I can't even express how good."

Without warning, Emma grabs me and pulls me into a huge hug. "I know we just met," she says when she finally lets me go, "but you have no idea how glad I am to see a fellow human. It's been so long."

"How long have you been here?" I ask, following her over to a pair of loveseats in the corner.

Pausing, she turns to one side and pulls her blue gown taut over her belly to outline the beginnings of a prominent baby bump. "At least this long," she says. Is there a note of resignation in her voice? "It's a bit hard to keep track of time here; I don't know whether they have the same number of hours in a day, or minutes in an hour... but I'd say a few months, at least." She moves to one of the sofas and indicates the other one. "Please, sit."

I sink down gratefully, then just stare at her. After what feels like forever being surrounded by nothing but Ulfarri, it's weird but somehow reassuring to be with another human woman. She seems tiny by comparison, and I realize that's how they must see me. "I have so many questions," I begin. "But I don't know how long we have."

"Most importantly, are you okay?" Her blue eyes are full of concern. "What exactly happened? How did you get here?"

I briefly outline waking up in the harem, and the weirdness that my life has been since. "A lot of my memories haven't come back yet." I shrug. "Maybe I had some kind of amnesia before I even got here."

"I'm so sorry," she says softly. "I tried to get Khan to convince them not to bring any human women over. I begged, I cried, I pleaded, I threatened. But surely you've been here long enough now to know how little influence we have if we want to make our mates do something they don't want."

My heart begins to pound, and there's a roaring of blood in my ears as I try to absorb this shocking bit of news. "You knew this was going to happen?" I manage.

Emma nods, sadly. "I overheard them talking about it. When the Ogsul put the Omega serum in me and it worked, the kings held a council and unilaterally decided to try it on their female Betas here. When that didn't take, they decided to get the magicians to find a way to bring more women from Earth. I swear, Kim, there was nothing I could do. Nothing."

I can see the genuine sorrow in her face, and a wave of pity floods me. "Of course there was nothing you could do. Did you try to escape?"

"Honestly? I didn't get a chance. I was in a cage, then on a spaceship, then on another spaceship, and then Khan stuck to me like white on rice, as you Americans say. He went through a phase where he didn't even put me down; just carried me everywhere like I was some kind of baby. And then, I fell in love with him."

"What?" I don't think I heard right.

"We went through a lot," Emma says, "and when I got the chance to leave, I realized I didn't want to. I wanted to stay here. With him."

"You got a chance to leave?" I seize on that little tidbit. "How?"

"He saw how unhappy I was. How much I missed Earth. He got the magicians to set up a portal so I could go home."

I lean back in the loveseat, my mind spinning with so many thoughts, I can barely get a grip on them. If they can set up a portal for her, they can set one up for me. If they've found a way to bring women here from Earth, they can send them back. Why didn't that occur to me before now? But Emma persuaded Khan to do that for her. There's no way I could get Aurus to do the same for me. "He would never."

"Huh?" Emma's blinking at me. "Who would never what?"

I realize I spoke aloud. "How did you get Khan to do

that for you? Aurus would never... I'd never be able to convince him to let me go back. Especially now that he's gotten rid of his harem."

"His harem?"

I briefly outline more details about what happened over the past couple of days, watching Emma's eyes get bigger and bigger. When I'm done, she bursts out laughing.

"Oh god," she giggles again, "I would have paid to have seen Aurus's face when he heard you'd taught them all to masturbate! And how could they not have ever worked that out themselves? Still, serves him right. Pompous—"

"—ass," I finish her sentence for her, but even as I say it, there's a flicker of something in my chest. "He is. Such a pompous ass. If only he wasn't so amazing in bed."

Emma's stopped laughing and now she's watching me curiously, her head cocked to one side. "I have to admit, I disliked Aurus on sight," she said. "When Khan took me to the Council of Kings, he was just so arrogant, so demanding... and all that ostentatious gold everywhere. Aside from the Stone King, he was probably my least favorite."

"Stone King?"

Emma shudders. "He's creepy as fuck. There are a bunch of kings here on Ulfaria. I assume you know?"

I nod. "One of the harem members clued me in to a lot of stuff. But I still don't really get the obsession with Omegas."

"Yeah, it took me a while to fully get that, too." Emma gets up and pours herself a glass of whatever's in the jug on the table. "Would you like a drink?"

"Sure." I accept the goblet gratefully, taking a long swallow of the cool, fragrant juice. "This is good!"

"Leeberry juice. I'm craving it. I mean, I'm craving

cheeseburgers more, but there just aren't any to be had around here." She settles back down into her blue couch, still clutching her goblet. "So, about the Omegas. Basically, this is how it works: Ulfarri society is made up of Alphas, Betas, and Omegas. This is like a caste system, and you're born into it. Betas make up the majority. They're the worker bees, the engineers, the scientists—or magicians, as they like to call them here," she gives a rueful little smile, "the artists... basically, most of the population. The Alphas are strong, bigger, and the warrior class, you could say. They're the protectors. The Omegas are essentially the breeders. Beta/Beta couples have Beta kids. In very rare instances, they'll have an Alpha or Omega baby, but it's rare enough that most people have never seen it happen. The army is dwindling, and the planet is constantly under threat from various other species who want to kill everyone here and take Ulfaria for themselves. Either for the resources, or just a new place to live. Ulfaria needs Alpha soldiers to stop that from happening. To make the next generation of Alphas, they need—"

"Omegas," I finish for her. "I remember Juno said that Alphas can't breed with Betas."

"Exactly." Emma sets her goblet down and curls up, pulling her legs underneath her.

"So the rut, the estrus, all the sex... essentially, Aurus is just trying to knock me up?"

"Afraid so. Believe me, I struggled with it. The last thing I ever wanted to do was have kids." She pats her belly and gives another rueful smile. "But after Khan..." She trails off, absorbed in her own thoughts.

"After Khan... what?" I prompt.

"It doesn't matter. I'll tell you another time. I don't know how long we have."

"Aurus doesn't know I have an IUD," I say quietly, and Emma's blue eyes widen.

"You do? Jesus, Kim! He'll lose his absolute shit!"

"I had it put in on Earth!" I'm indignant, wondering why I feel so defensive. "It's not like I knew I was coming here!"

"You're right, of course." She covers her mouth but a giggle escapes anyway. "God, I'd love to see his face when you tell him."

I snicker. "I'm waiting for the right moment." I waggle my brows.

"Aurus isn't going to know what hit him. I'm glad you're comfortable standing up to him. I get the impression that few people—if any—do."

"Yeah, he tells me all the time: *You are not what I expected.*"

"Maybe that's a good thing." Emma's gaze grows penetrating. "So you are settling in with him okay?"

"For now. I'm not planning on staying with him. I'm going to escape," I tell her.

"And go where? It's not easy to get back to Earth."

"I don't need to go back to Earth," I say, and it's true. I have no specific memories of my home on Earth, why would I want to return? Besides, Ulfaria is so fascinating. "Anywhere. Leave the palace. Go exploring. Teach sexual liberation classes to Beta women, I don't know."

Emma giggles again. "Oh, Aurus will love that."

"Yeah, he doesn't get a say," I announce with more boldness than I feel. "I was hoping you could help me."

Emma considers this, twisting her fingers together in her lap. "Is Aurus unkind to you?"

The question takes me completely by surprise. "Well, he's not cruel. He doesn't keep me naked and chained to a wall somewhere." My pussy pulses when I imagine it—apparently, it thinks being at Aurus's mercy would be hot. "He's even almost tender, at times. But that's not the point. I'm still a prisoner, even if I do have scented baths and pretty dresses..." *And shaking orgasms, and protective cuddles.* "It's the best sex I've ever had, or probably will ever have. But it's not enough."

Emma is quiet for some time, still twisting her fingers. "I wish I could help you," she says, "I really do, but I don't see how. Unless we somehow convince Aurus to send you away. I mean, I could help you escape from him, but I doubt he'd just let you go."

"Maybe I could hide out here?" As soon as I suggest it, I realize how dumb the question is.

Emma presses her lips together.

I wave a hand at her. "Just say it."

"That might start a war," she says gently. "And I am now queen of my people. I am responsible for the safety of my kingdom."

I blink at the sudden regality in her tone. This petite human really is a queen.

"If it were just me, it'd be different. But..." She pats her belly.

"No, of course. Silly me."

"You could try to go back to Earth, but it would take some doing. The magicians know how to do it, but it's difficult and can go wrong. And they're loyal to the kings, so that'd be a hard sell."

"What about a spaceship?" I can't sit still, so I rise and start pacing. Emma regards me from her seat.

"That's a possibility. But even if you had one, even if you could pilot it—or get someone else to—how would you find Earth? You wouldn't know where to start. And anyone who was found to be helping you…"

The rest of the sentence hangs in the air, heavy as lead. Anyone found to be helping me would be killed. Aurus has already said as much.

"I guess even getting out of the palace will be difficult. Aurus isn't the type to just let me go. His precious Omega…" I mock, but there's a pang in my heart. It wouldn't be so bad to stay with Aurus—the sex is amazing. Golden dick is great—it just sucks that it's attached to the rest of him. Maybe a gag…

Emma's watching me, a soft expression on her face. I rub my forehead. For some reason, I had pinned all my hopes on her, and now the utter futility of my situation is hitting me like a baseball bat to the face.

"Fuck," I say softly.

"I'm sorry."

"It's not your fault. I can make the best of this situation. That's just the sort of person I am. I just want a few more choices." I cross to the table and snatch up a cookie looking thing. Instead of taking a bite, I crumble it between my fingers.

"It'll be okay," she says. "We'll figure something out. I might not be able to help you escape, but I'm sure there are other things I can do for you." She leans back in her loveseat and regards me, little twin lines between her brows.

"You've already been a huge help," I tell her. It's true. It must have been awful for her, being entirely alone in her situation for as long as she was. "But yeah. Maybe we can find a way to… if not prevent more women from being taken from Earth, at least help them when they get here."

"What I want to know is how they select the women," Emma says, looking thoughtful. "I mean, I fell through the portal accidentally, as far as I know. But Aurus requested a blonde, and..." She gestures at my head, and I run my hand over my shaggy hair.

"I kind of hacked it off." I grin. "To annoy him."

Her smile makes her eyes light up. "That's hilarious! Did it work?"

"Oh yeah. He was furious." Still, her words are making me think. "You need to grill Khan," I say slowly. "I get the impression you have a much deeper relationship with him than I do with Aurus, who sees me as nothing but a courtesan."

"That's kind of how Khan treated me at first too," Emma admits. "The bond developed later on, though he did give me the claiming bite very early."

"Claiming bite? He fucking *bit* you?"

"Something in my scent told him I was his soul mate, and then he bit my neck during the rut, binding me to him. Since then, we can feel each other's emotions. Hard to describe, and very bizarre. But it definitely made us grow closer." She slides her long, golden mane aside to show a circular scar on her neck, right where it meets her shoulder.

"Ouch. Looks like it was painful." My neck twinges in sympathy and I clamp a hand over it.

"It was... but for one thing, I kind of get off on pain. And for another... he did it during sex, so..." she trails off, little dots of pink staining her cheeks.

"Do you think Aurus will do that to me?" I'm still holding my neck. Gah. I drop back into my seat and knot my hands into my lap.

She shrugs. "I don't know. Khan talked like the soul bond is some special kind of thing, so maybe not everyone has it. It didn't sound like every Alpha/Omega pairing is the same."

"Soul bond?"

"Mmmhmm." She covers her face with a hand. "It's a thing Alpha and Omega couples sometimes share. It's, um, it's more than a connection. It happens here..." She drops her hand and taps her chest, right over her heart. "I don't even know how to describe it. Imagine all the happiness in the world, but like as a connection between you and your mate. You feel everything—good, bad, ugly—but you'll feel it together, and there's this... I don't know, satisfaction that lives perpetually between you. It's like coming home."

"That sounds amazing. At the same time, it doesn't sound like something Aurus would want. A connection with another being? He's all about himself."

"It is amazing," Emma agrees in her soft, kind voice. "But like I said, not every couple has it."

"Interesting." I try to sound nonchalant. There's no reason for me to feel sad. It's not like I want to be connected with Aurus that way, either. Right? "I guess we'll see how things go. Aside from being in bed, we haven't done anything else together. Nothing to forge any kind of connection. I sleep away from him, in the harem HQ. So maybe he does just see me as a walking womb."

"It's so infuriating, isn't it? To be reduced to that? Like we don't have thoughts, feelings, desires of our own." She looks around at her gorgeous studio. "I'm lucky to have all this now. But it was a long road to get here."

"This palace is stunning, from what I've seen," I tell her, following her gaze to the astounding view of waterfalls and trees. "Have you learned to pilot those zooming platforms?"

"The skimmers? I have! It's such fun!"

"I still haven't worked out the doors yet, though. How do they open? Is it some kind of password? Hidden button? I don't see the servants touching anything."

"Oh, it's easy! I'll show you." She gets up and moves over to the door. "Come on!"

I follow her. If I know how to open the doors, it will be a lot easier to escape Aurus and his stupid golden palace—if only for a while.

"There's a hidden tile in front of every door here," Emma says, indicating it with her foot. "If you look closely, you can see it's a teeny bit more raised than the rest of them. The tile is always on the left hand side, and all you have to do is step on it. Like this." She takes a step forward and the door glides open.

"Really? That's all?"

"To close it, you just tap it again. Or you make sure to walk on the one on the other side as you go through," she adds.

"Well, that's a lot easier than I thought. Thank you!"

She turns her gaze to me, her expression suddenly serious. "We have to do something about the women from Earth," she says. "I can talk to Khan, but we need to work out some kind of game plan first. A list of requests, or questions, even, to start with. I mean, what if they brought over a woman who has young kids back home? Or someone who needs regular medical treatment? Someone who's caring for elderly parents or, hell, who just has a pet!"

Now that she's mentioning it, I see how right she is. "On the other hand, I bet there'd be women willing to sign up for this kind of thing voluntarily if they had the chance," I say. "I mean, regular amazing sex and the chance to be an actual queen... someone who's miserable on Earth, someone who's trying to escape her circumstances..."

"I see what you mean. Okay, let's sit down and try to work something out. It's easy to lose track of time here but I can't see Khan and Aurus leaving us alone for much longer."

As I follow her back to the loveseats, I feel something new and exciting budding in my heart.

Hope.

THIRTEEN

Aurus

ONCE KIM HAS LEFT to go see Emma, Khan leads me to his audience chamber. I follow him, easily matching his fast, confident stride. I look around me as we pass through rooms and walk along hallways, curious about his inner sanctum.

I've never been this far inside his palace before. It is far inferior to mine, of course. No gold anywhere. It's very understated, with muted colors, and sleek lines and architecture. Bright, stunning paintings adorn the walls, the white canvases filled with vibrant, moving shapes.

"Emma did most of them," Khan says over his shoulder. "She has an affinity for art."

"It would seem she does," I reply, not sure what else to say. "Was this something she discovered here, or was it always the case?"

"She was an artist back on Earth too. Here we are." Khan sinks onto a huge, silver brocade sofa and raises a hand. Immediately, a servant appears. "Refreshments, please," he says, and the Beta scurries away. "But I hired an artist to show her how to use Ulfarri paints and the magic dust."

"Very indulgent of you," I say, taking a seat in a sumptuous armchair opposite him. "I suppose it's good to keep them occupied."

Khan regards me with narrowed eyes. "It's her passion," he says. "And it gives me joy to support her in that."

There's a brief moment of tension in the air. Khan and I always had a stilted relationship, but our last meetings were even less friendly, since he had just claimed his Omega and was insanely protective of her. "That's nice," I say dismissively. "I suppose she will be too busy once she gives birth."

"She will still paint as much as she can," Khan says, still glowering at me. Really, you'd think I was insulting him somehow from the way he's acting.

"I'm sure."

There's an awkward silence and I compose myself, trying to remember all the things I wanted to ask him.

"Are all Hoo-mans defiant and unruly?" Might as well start with the most burning question of all.

Khan regards me with what can only be described as bemusement. "Emma had her moments when we first met, but I believe anyone would react badly to circumstances such as the ones she found herself in."

I let that sink in. "Kim is not what I expected at all. She keeps threatening to escape."

This time, an actual chuckle is Khan's response. "And how do you respond?"

"I don't take it seriously," I admit. "After all, she has nowhere to go. And even if she did manage to get out of the palace, there's nowhere on Ulfaria where I wouldn't find her."

"True," Khan muses, "although if I were you, I'd be

worried about her straying into another kingdom. Some kings will not hesitate to take her for their own, especially at the moment, before we have enough Omegas for all."

Hot, prickly rage travels up my spine and makes my every nerve ending tingle. "They would not dare," I growl. "I would kill every last one."

Khan raises a palm. "Settle down," he says, "going in and out of the rut is making you more aggressive than usual."

"That's true." The Beta returns with drinks and I take some wine, sipping it gratefully. "I learned that the hard way when she appeared in the training arena while I was there with several dozen Alpha soldiers."

Khan leans forward, almost dropping his goblet. "What happened?"

I tell him, not missing the way his face darkens.

"A close escape," he says when I've finished. "That could have ended a lot worse."

"I've tried punishing her," I admit, "but I cannot watch her all of the time. I have a kingdom to run. And now I've sent my harem away... not that they were very good at stopping her in the first place. When Kim decides she wants something..."

"Hoo-man females react differently to punishment," Khan tells me. "According to Emma, they are equal to males in every way on Earth. Besides," his lips quirk up in a grin, "Emma is unusual in that she enjoys the way I punish her. I discovered very early on that pain arouses her."

I stare at him, hardly believing my ears. "I think this would be a good time to remind you that anything shared in this conversation is to remain in strict confidence," I say.

"Agreed."

"So how do you punish her if she enjoys the usual ways?" I ask.

"I no longer have need to punish her, aside from the occasional bit of role play for fun," he says. "We are quite content."

I want that, I realize. I want Kim to be content with me, to obey me, to be mine as Emma is so obviously—and voluntarily—Khan's. "She is no longer unhappy? How did you achieve that?"

Khan takes a long swallow of wine and pushes his mane of hair over his shoulder before answering. "We still have disagreements, but when I offered to send her home, she realized she wants to stay. She finally felt the soul bond."

"I still cannot believe you offered to send her home." I shake my head. The thought of losing Kim makes my skin crawl. "I don't know why you did it."

"I would do anything for her," Khan says quietly. "When I gave her the claiming bite, it bound me to her such that I could—can—almost feel her emotions. She was sad all the time. It was not to be borne. That is why I directed the magicians to find a way to send her back to Earth. I was going to go with her, of course, as my life no longer has meaning without her in it."

I rub my chest. I understand the sentiment, but I don't like it. Khan speaks as if he is a part of a whole, but he is not lesser for making his Omega his equal. He is more.

"As you know, I didn't have a high probability of surviving the trip through the portal," he continues, "but it was a risk I was willing to take. At the last moment, she decided she couldn't go. She wanted to stay. She chose me."

Never in my life before have I envied anyone the way I envy Khan in this moment.

"Incredible," I murmur. I must find a way to make Kim

choose me. "And when did you decide to give Emma the claiming bite?"

Khan's piercing gaze seems to go straight through me, making me uncomfortable. "It wasn't a conscious decision," he says. "I knew from her scent that she was my soul mate, and when we were rutting, my canines lengthened, and I... I just did it."

Suddenly, all I want is to get Kim, take her back to Aurum, and do the same with her. I want her to be mine in all ways.

"How are the magicians coming along in their quest to bring more Hoo-mans here?" Khan continues, setting down his empty goblet and leaning back. "Have there been any others aside from Kim?"

I sigh. "Truth be told, I haven't been following their progress as closely as I should. I've been... distracted by other things." Honestly, I don't much care whether they find other Omegas. I have mine now. I want to focus all my attention on her.

"That's a shame," Khan says lightly. "Emma will have questions. She still begs me not to allow it."

"Allow what? More Hoo-man females to be brought here?" I scoff. "That is none of her concern."

"She would disagree with you there," Khan says. The fond tone in his voice whenever he speaks of Emma is undeniable. "Surely you would rescue fellow Ulfarri, should you deem them to be in danger?"

"We treat the Hoo-mans well," I say. "They are not in any danger."

Khan rubs his chin. "Not from us, perhaps," he muses, "but would you vouch for all the other kings? Even the ones who do not make up the Council Nine? Could you guarantee that none of the Hoo-mans would be in danger should they find themselves out in Ulfarian wilderness? Or amongst rogue Alphas?"

He has a point. "But we must bring more in," I argue. "We have an entire army to rebuild and sustain. Never forget, Ulfaria has many enemies. It has been decades since we've been badly attacked, but the warning systems have flagged up unusual activity in Chitin territory."

"Then we need to make sure we are prepared," Khan says. "Call the council to alert the kings. If the Chitin dare enter our atmosphere, they will face the wrath of the Brutal Ones. If they even can get close. Our planet now has more defenses than ever."

"And if those defenses fail?"

"I have my Sky Fighters. And you have your army. None can stand against the Aurum Alphas."

It's a blatant compliment obviously spoken to flatter me, but it works. "They are well trained," I say proudly. "Still, we both know it is not this generation that lacks Alpha soldiers. It will be the next generation—unless we do what is necessary to change that."

"And we will," Khan promises, "but I wish to be more involved in that process. As does Emma. She knows Earth, she knows Hoo-mans. She is a great resource."

"She will whine, or plead, or do anything else she can think of to stop us," I counter. "I do not think involving her would be wise."

"Leave that up to me," Khan says. "Meanwhile, I think you should be more focused on Kim, and doing what you can to make her happy. I've come to believe that Hoo-man females are more likely to conceive when they are happy."

I raise an incredulous eyebrow. "I suspect that may be something Emma told you in order to ensure she always gets her own way."

His sudden outrage is visible in Khan's tense shoulders. "She does not always get her own way," he snaps, "but I do derive pleasure from seeing her content. If Kim is being unruly and refusing to submit, I would suggest you try giving her something she wants."

"Like what?" My hackles are raised at the implication that I am not pleasing my Omega, and I'm struggling to suppress my fury.

Khan shrugs. "For Emma, it was painting. For Kim... who knows? Just ask her."

"Perhaps I shall." I get up from the armchair, signaling that our audience is over. My thoughts are full of Kim. It's getting harder and harder for me to be apart from her.

Soon, I must give her the claiming bite and complete the soul bond. I want to feel close to her. I want to be inside her always.

My cock is throbbing in my breeches. "Please send someone to fetch Kim. It is time for us to go home."

FOURTEEN

Kim

I'M BORED. So, so bored. For some reason, I thought things would change after we visited Khan and Emma.

I was wrong.

As soon as we returned to Aurum, Aurus took me into his chambers and fucked me until neither of us could move. Then, at some point, I fell asleep, and he left.

I haven't seen him since. I don't know how long he's been gone, but I'm alone in his chambers. Servants bring me food and drink, and in between mealtimes, I doze, I take baths in his vast tub, and I pace. I've cut off the bottoms of all my fancy gowns so I can stride unencumbered. Sometimes I do little workout routines, trying to recapture the fighting and acrobatic knowledge I seem to have. I wish Aurus would let me onto the training grounds, so I can really see what I can do. I only brought it up once, and he shot me right down.

I'm still his little Omega pet. Nothing more, nothing less.

My entire conversation with Emma replays over and over in my mind. They're bringing more human women over to Ulfaria. We have to stop it. There are portals. I could go back... if I wanted. Emma persuaded Khan. Could I do the same with Aurus? Is that what I want?

I had hoped to get a chance to talk to him, to get a read on how he feels about it all. To maybe help him see my side. To at least convince him that it would be better to somehow get volunteers to sign up to come, rather than randomly snatching women off the streets on Earth.

But I have no idea where he is, or when he's coming back. The servants won't talk to me. They bring me refreshments and glide away again, careful not to say a word. And none of them are male. Aurus is still uber-protective of me, it seems.

Some of the harem members may have been insanely full of themselves, but at least we had conversations. I asked whether I could go visit them in the city, but was given a brusque *no* as reply.

I'm lonely.

Eventually, I've had enough. I need to get out of here. Some fresh air might do me good. I pull on the warmest gown I can find—Aurus provided a selection for me—and a pair of shoes. They're soft, supple leather of some kind, and it feels like I'm not wearing any at all. There don't seem to be phones on this planet, but they do have some comforts I adore.

Raising my chin, adopting a queenly attitude, I step on the tile to open the main door and stride through it as if I don't have a care in the world. I'm expecting there to be soldiers guarding the entrance... but there aren't any. How strange.

How convenient.

In Aurus's main hall, where I first met him, I glance up at the wall full of weapons, chewing my lip. Should I try to climb up and steal one?

No. I'm not going anywhere to fight. I'm just heading out for some air. I don't want to give Aurus a reason to be mad at me when he does return.

I walk until I find more doors, vaguely remembering the path to outside from when the girls took me to the training arena. The palace seems eerily quiet and subdued. Where is everyone? There's a weird vibe that makes me slightly uneasy, but I decide to ignore it. I can't be in any danger. As protective as Aurus is, there's no way he'd leave me alone if there was any kind of threat.

I find the huge, ornate doors that lead outside and, sure enough, there's a hidden tile to open them. I step on it and head out.

This time, there are helmeted soldiers on the other side... but even though they turn their heads and obviously see me, they don't call out or try to stop me. I'm surprised but beyond relieved. The warmth of the suns on my skin feels amazing, and I head around a corner, trying to decide where to go.

When I see the row of zooming platforms lined up, my heart starts to beat faster, and I'm genuinely excited for the first time in what feels like days. I could go for a ride. I'd be safe from weird, alien animals on one of those things, and could still do some exploring. Aurus showed me how to work the joystick, and it didn't look that hard.

I step on and watch the lights blink on the control pad. The platform wobbles a bit, like when you step onto a boat, but it's big enough and sturdy enough that I don't think it will crash to the ground.

Pushing the biggest button makes the joystick light up

and I wrap my hand around it cautiously, taking a deep breath before moving it forward just a tiny bit.

Sure enough, the platform begins to glide out of the dock.

Soon, I work out the various directions, and discover that lifting the stick makes the platform rise higher in the air, while pushing it down makes the platform sink lower.

This is fun!

Once I've gotten a feel for the controls, I set off on a little tour to explore some of the area outside the palace. A bunch of cow-looking creatures stare at me as I glide by, and I marvel at their size, wondering if they're dangerous. Everything on this planet seems bigger than on Earth: its inhabitants, its flora and fauna...

"The dicks," I mutter, thinking about Aurus. "Everything's bigger in Ulfaria..."

Chuckling to myself at my bad joke, I almost jump out of my skin at a nearby roar.

"Kim!"

Turning, I see Aurus approaching on a zooming platform of his own.

"Kim! What in Ulf's name are you doing? Get back here!" He's obviously livid, his burnt honey eyes flashing.

"I was *bored*!" I yell back.

"You're trying to escape! There is no escape!"

Suddenly, I'm filled with anger. How dare he? The asshole leaves me alone for days and then, when I'm finally having some fun, he appears out of nowhere, tries to stop me, and makes unfair accusations. "I'm not!" I retort, turning my back on him and pushing the joystick forward to accelerate.

"We need to get back to the palace, now!"

Such a killjoy. Looking over my shoulder, I see he's

going faster now, too, and impulsively, I decide I won't let him spoil my good time. "Catch me if you can!" I laugh, then zoom away from him, turning a precarious circle and shooting away.

"Oh, I'll catch you! And when I do—"

The rest of his words get lost in the whistling sound of the wind as I speed off, ducking and weaving around trees, enjoying the speed and thrill of the chase, proud of how fast I was able to get a handle on steering this thing.

He's behind me, of course—though I don't dare turn around to look, I can sense his proximity, and the occasional whiff of his intoxicating scent fills my nostrils.

"Where are you going?" he calls out.

"Anywhere but here! I hate you!" I blurt, pushing the joystick until I'm traveling as fast as I dare.

"You still hate me?" The hurt in his voice takes me by surprise. Then it makes me mad. I've told him over and over, and even when I think I might care for him a little, he proves how little I mean to him. How full of himself he is.

How I'm nothing more than his little pet.

"Fuck that," I whisper, and push the joystick all the way forward. Full throttle. The skimmer gives a lurch, almost leaving my heart behind me. Crap, that's fast—

"Kim, watch out!"

At the note of panic in his tone, I look back at Aurus—there's a blaze of agony, then everything goes dark...

When I open my eyes, Aurus's handsome, golden face swims into focus. He's on his knees, cradling me, his eyes bright with worry. "Little Omega," he croons.

"Ow." I put a hand to my forehead to feel the beginnings of what will undoubtedly be a spectacular lump.

"You didn't see the tree?"

"I didn't see the damn tree," I admit wryly.

"Are you hurt?"

"I don't think so." I do a quick scan of my body, wiggling my fingers and toes. Aside from the throbbing bump on my head, I seem to be fine.

"What were you thinking?" The worry in his tone has turned to accusation, and another wave of anger flares up in me.

"I was *bored*!" I struggle in his hold, trying to get up, but his brute strength keeps me pinned in place. "You left me alone for days! Completely alone! Not a word about where you were, or what you were doing! Nobody for company or conversation... nothing to do but think. I wanted to get out and explore!"

There's a pause. "You were not trying to escape?"

"You said it yourself," I mutter, "there is no escape."

"Ulf," he says, "when I saw you hit that branch..." He crushes me to him and I realize he's gently kissing the top of my head.

"Let go of me!" I don't want him to be kind or tender right now. I'm too mad.

"Never, never," he says. "You are mine, Kim. I was so worried. I will never leave you alone again."

"Where did you go, anyway?" I lean back far enough to be able to see his face. It's shuttered. I sense that he's hiding something from me.

"I had business with the council, but it doesn't matter now. What matters is that you are not hurt. Oh, my little Omega, I—" His lips find mine and he's kissing me hard, his tongue plundering my mouth, drinking down my protests.

His scent is filling my nostrils, new leather and sandalwood, making me dizzy with need, and my arms reach up as if I have no control over them, clinging to him like I'm drowning and he's my life line.

Why do I want him so much? I'm torn between anger and desire, and when his big hand slides down to cup my sex, his palm grinding against my clit, I gush, moaning into his kiss.

He's growling now, licking down my neck and pushing me down until I'm lying on my back, then nudging my legs apart with his huge thigh.

A faraway part of my brain wonders whether he's using sex to comfort me, then the familiar stretching, throbbing sensation of his cock sliding up inside me robs me of all coherent thought.

Aurus is thrusting deep and slow, hitting me in all the right places, and my climax is thundering towards me with all the subtlety of a freight train. I can sense that something's different... there's an underlying note of tenderness in him... and his low, bitonal growl is raising goosebumps on my flesh.

I spread my thighs wider and run my fingers through his thick, gold hair, raking his scalp with my nails.

Rearing up, he lets out a roar and the knot forms, searing my pussy, tipping me over the edge.

Squeezing my eyes shut, I lose myself in my orgasm, wave after wave of pleasure making my core contract around him.

A sharp, blinding pain in my neck makes me gasp, and my eyes fly open.

He's biting me, his canines sinking deep into the soft place where my neck meets my shoulder.

The claiming bite.

It hurts so good. The sizzle of pain turns to pleasure in my core.

His enormous body covers me. I push at his chest before he crushes me.

Might as well be trying to move a mountain.

His thick forearm slides across my chest, pinning me down as he sucks and licks the wound.

I shudder with aftershocks with each lick.

"Fuck," I mumble. I sound drunk. "Aurus..."

"Mine," he purrs. "We are bonded now." He rears up and looks down at me with those intense, hypnotizing, amber eyes. "Now you belong to me. Forever."

There's a twinge of sadness deep in my chest, followed by a jolt of helpless anger. Better to be mad than hurt. "Whatever," I whisper.

It's true. I'll always belong to him. But the thought brings me nothing but pain.

No matter how much I love him, he won't ever be mine.

FIFTEEN

Aurus

Words cannot describe the horror I felt when I saw that huge orange branch collide with Kim's head. My heart stopped beating, all the breath left my lungs, and my entire focus narrowed down to one thing: making sure she was unhurt.

In that instant, I knew with piercing certainty that I love her.

I love her.

So once we had ascertained that she'd had a lucky escape, my only instinct was to claim her. To make her mine in every way.

Forever.

Her howl of anguish when my teeth sank into her soft, peach flesh chilled my bones but there was nothing I could do. I was too far gone in the rut and besides, it had to be done.

After my conversation with Khan, I had thought about

giving her the claiming bite more and more—but something had still held me back. Kim is defiant. She is infuriating. She does not want to be with me.

When she shouted at me that she hates me, zooming away from me on that platform, it felt like a poison-tipped dagger spearing me in the chest.

And that only fueled my desire for her.

Now, with the taste of her tingling on my tongue, my loins exploding with pleasure as I shoot into her over and over, I know I did the right thing.

Kim was destined to be my mate.

We have a soul bond, and now that I've claimed her, she will feel it too. She will no longer be relegated to a mere harem. She will be my equal in every way, always by my side, as it should be.

I slump over her, breathing in her sweet musk, feeling more alive than after the fiercest battle. My heart is pounding so hard, it takes a moment to register that my little Omega is shaking beneath me.

I rub my cheek against hers, scent marking her. Her wispy hair tickles me. I love how it frames her pixie-like face. Did I ever hate how she cut it short? Now I cannot imagine it any other way. It suits her.

She is nothing like a typical Omega, but that makes her all the more precious.

With great effort, I lift myself up enough that I can look down into her face.

She looks almost... sad. Then she clocks me watching her, and her features harden.

"Motherfucker!" she spits, her beautiful green eyes wide with an expression I cannot interpret. "You *bit* me!"

"I am sorry it hurt you, little Omega," I murmur,

pressing a kiss to her smooth forehead, "but it had to be done. We are bonded now. We belong together."

"Like hell!" She struggles beneath my weight, her little fists pummeling my back. Resistance is futile, when will she learn that? "Get off of me!"

"Only if you promise not to run." Her skimmer was wrecked when she crashed it, so her only option would be to steal mine. I'd like to think she wouldn't dare, but she would. The guards I had posted outside the palace obeyed their orders and notified me as soon as they saw her walking out. They said she didn't seem to be in a hurry, and might just be going for a stroll, but I knew the truth. She was trying to make good her constant threats to escape.

"For the last time, asshole, I wasn't running away! I was exploring!"

I am used to deference and respect, and Kim's insults only serve to remind me how different she is from Ulfarri females. From a proper Omega. "Watch your words," I say sternly, slowly extricating my cock from her and tucking it back into my breeches before rising to a crouch and offering her my hand.

She ignores it, scrambling to her feet without my help. "I'll say what I like! Jesus!" Her fingers go to the wound on her neck. "Is it bleeding?" Her voice has softened, and the sudden switch from adorable fury to abject vulnerability makes my heart clench in my chest.

"No," I tell her gently. "I cleaned it carefully, and will bandage it when we're back at the palace."

"You licked it," she mutters. "That wasn't cleaning it."

"The claiming bite is a biological process," I explain. "There are healing and antibacterial properties in my saliva."

"Oh."

"Still, you shouldn't touch it." I reach out and take her hand from her shoulder, clasping her palm. My huge hand swallows hers as I lead her to the skimmer. "We should return. It's getting late." Indeed, the suns are sinking lower, toward the horizon.

"You still didn't tell me where you were this whole time," she says quietly, "and I'm still mad at you for leaving me."

Should I tell her the truth? That I was called to an emergency council meeting with the other kings, as we recently received word that enemy ships were spotted heading towards Ulfaria? "I will explain once we are home," I say, deciding that this is neither the time, nor the place. I need her back in my bed, safe.

Stepping onto the skimmer, I tug her alongside me and wrap a possessive arm around her waist, taking the controls with my other hand.

"I'm sorry I crashed mine," Kim mutters. She is not actively pulling away from me, nor is she leaning in. I'm struggling to interpret her thoughts. Strange. Khan said I would be able to feel her emotions through the bond once I had claimed her.

"No matter," I say. "The important thing is that you're not hurt—aside from that nasty bump on your head, which I will have the magicians look at."

"And the nasty bite on my neck," she adds. Her pretty little face is set in a scowl.

"Again, I am sorry that hurt, but it was necessary." I draw the joystick up and slide it forward before turning us around so we can head home.

"Why? You don't care about me! I'm just a walking womb to you."

"That is untrue!" Outrage makes my voice loud, and I force myself to reel it back, to remain calm. "Why do you think that?"

"I don't think it, I know it. Juno and the others said as much, as did Emma. You need an Omega to breed with. It doesn't matter what she's like as a person. Her thoughts, feelings, happiness, are irrelevant. You don't involve me in anything—I'm just your Omega pet. You don't care about me once you're done rutting me. You tell me I'm a disappointment as an Omega—"

"When did I say that?"

"*You're not what I expected, Kim,*" she bites off in a high-pitched mockery of my voice.

"Well, you are not..." I start, and stop when her eyes blaze with livid fire. "But you are not a disappointment."

"You don't mean that," she scoffs. "You don't have to say it—you showed it. I don't mean anything to you. You rut me, and then leave me like a dog in a cage. The second I stop behaving like a perfect little Omega, you send me back to the harem."

Every word of her tirade is like a needle to my heart. It's true. Her stubborn defiance and lack of respect made it easy for me to focus on her status as an Omega, nothing more. But something has changed since then. How to explain it? "I may have treated you that way in the beginning," I concede, steering us through a copse of trees, relieved when the glittering palace appears, shimmering in the distance, "but you made it hard to get to know you as a person. All you did was disobey me, and talk of escape."

"You still treat me that way." Her tone is resigned now, and that's somehow worse than when she's yelling at me. "You left me alone. Again. No explanation, no warning. I'm not just some slave to be used for pleasure and then set aside and ignored when you want a break. I have feelings."

I tighten my hold on her, inhaling the sweet scent of her hair. For the first time, I can feel our bond. There is sorrow throbbing through it. It damn near breaks my heart. "Please forgive me," I tell her. "Let's discuss everything when we return. And I'll explain where I went when I left you."

She lets out a little sigh, and there's silence for a while. I'm in a hurry to get home but I don't want to risk crashing the skimmer, so I force myself to maintain a safe speed.

At last, the golden road stretches before us, gleaming in the glow cast by the setting suns. My palace is looming ever bigger up ahead.

"There's something I need to tell you, too," Kim says. "You're not going to like it."

"Tell me."

"Not now, while you're driving. Later, when we talk."

Something in her tone makes the hackles rise on the back of my neck. A prickle of panic. An impending sense of doom. I can feel her fear through the bond. Suddenly desperate to know, I shift the platform to a halt just a few inches above the golden road and turn her to face me, my hands on her shoulders. "Tell me now," I say, the command inherent in my voice.

She looks away. "I... I won't give you heirs," she says slowly. "I can't."

Did I hear that right? "What?" I croak.

"I can't get pregnant!" she says, meeting my gaze at last. Her expression is defiant, defensive. "I have an IUD."

"What?" She's not making sense. I only just resist the urge to shake her.

"On Earth," now she's talking slowly and deliberately,

as if I were some kind of simpleton, "I had a device put in me that stops me from getting pregnant. It's called an IUD."

The mere idea of this is ridiculous. Why would anyone do such a thing? What would be the point? Ignoring the roaring of blood in my ears, I swallow once, and try to remain calm. "Why?"

She shrugs. "Lots of women use birth control when they don't want to get pregnant."

"Why wouldn't they want to get pregnant?"

Another shrug. "Loads of different reasons. Not meeting the right guy yet. Being too young. Wanting to focus on a career—"

"This device, this... FID?"

"IUD," she corrects me.

"Can it be removed? Reversed?"

"Yes. By a doctor. On Earth. It's in my womb. I can't take it out myself."

Suddenly, I see what she's doing. She's lying to me. This is an elaborate ploy to get me to allow her to return to Earth, ostensibly to have this thing removed. Luckily, I can see right through it. "Nice try," I say.

"Huh?" There's genuine puzzlement on her face.

"If you have such a thing, the magicians will find a way to remove it safely. You do not need to return to Earth. You belong here. With me."

"What if I don't want it removed?" Wrenching herself out of my hold and taking a step back, she folds her arms across her chest.

I snort. "You do not have a choice."

"Don't I?"

I can feel her anger thrumming in our bond. "No," I snarl, my own temper rising. "You belong to me." Must she fight me at every turn? I move to take her shoulders, then see her eyes widen as she gazes at something behind me. In the bond, her anger has turned into icy cold terror, dripping down my spine, and I know what's happening even before the shadow slides over her face, blanketing us both.

I must get Kim to safety.

We are under attack.

SIXTEEN

Kim

"What is it?" I ask. "What's happening?"

Aurus's face has contorted into a grim mask. A shadow has fallen over us. The sky has turned dark with huge black spaceships blotting out the suns. There are so many.

"The Chitin are here." His voice is grim.

The wind has picked up, cold air cutting through the heat. The air turns bitter with a sulfuric scent. My skin prickles.

"We must go," Aurus says, tugging me up against him and putting a protective arm around me. I grab onto him as he throttles forward, pushing the skimmer to its limit. We zoom down the golden road to the palace. Instead of heading to the huge front doors, we zip up to a tall tower and land on the flat surface. Winds blast over us, tearing at my gown.

"There is no time," Aurus mutters. His face wears a hard expression. He lifts me up and leaps off the skimmer, his movements fluid but spare. "Kim." He sets me down and steadies me with his hands on my shoulders. "You must go down..." He nods to a small opening leading to what I assume is a staircase. "You must hide yourself."

"Okay." I swallow. "But what are you going to do?"

"I must go into battle. The enemy is here."

Overhead, rows of ships blanket every available inch of sky. They're just hovering there... what are they doing? "But—"

Go!" He gives me a push, and I scuttle to the stairs. A few steps down, I stop and peek out to see what Aurus is doing.

There's a guardhouse on top of this tower. Aurus runs up to the wall and punches the side. Some sort of invisible button triggers the wall to make it open, revealing a huge, golden suit of armor. It looks like his regular armor, but bigger.

He presses the breastplate and the armor sections open wide enough for him to slide inside. In seconds, his seven foot tall form has been transformed into a ten foot tall armored superhero version of an Alpha. There's a mechanical hum from his suit as he strides to the edge of the tower. He pauses, and turns back to me.

"Go down, Kim," he commands. "Follow the stairs to the lowest levels. The Betas will guide you to the bunker." And he leaps off the edge into the air.

I gasp. I'm about to run over and see if he fell, where he fell, when he zooms back into sight. The air under his booted feet ripples from some sort of hovercraft tech.

"Kim!" he barks. "I need you to obey me. I need you to be safe."

"What about you?" I call against the wind whipping over my head.

"I will fight. I am an Alpha. It is what I do." He's

gaining elevation now, floating overhead. He turns, and zooms away.

Straight for the line of alien craft.

"Oh my god." I race over to the edge. Aurus's golden shape glimmers in the shadow of the enemy. Is he going to fight those big ships all by himself?

I know he has a huge ego, but come on. He's going to take on fifty ships a million times bigger than him?

Aurus stretches out his arms, still hovering in the air. He's the perfect target. I hold my breath, waiting for the ships to fire on him and incinerate him to dust.

My heart clenches. I don't want that to happen.

Bong! A familiar sound makes me jump.

Down in the arena, someone's banging the gong. Dang, that thing does carry. Shouts echo up the stairwell. Hopefully, everyone's going to hide. There are a ton of people in this palace. Alpha soldiers, Beta magicians, all the servants. I hope they'll stay safe.

Maybe I should go help them. Go with them. But I can't. I can't do what Aurus asked, what he ordered me to, not while he's up there, facing the enemy all alone.

He's still just hanging in the air, a bright dot against the enemy's hulls.

My jaw aches from gritting my teeth.

This is insane.

Bong! Something creaks, then groans. The whole palace trembles. I grab onto the wall to steady myself. A thunderous marching sound makes me look down. Over to the right, the golden road stretches from the columned front. The five-story high palace doors have opened, and row upon row of soldiers are marching out in perfect formation: huge Alphas in golden suits like their king's.

They march down the road to where it widens, then

halt. Rank by rank, they launch their hovergear and take to the sky, zooming up to join their king.

Yes!

I punch the top of the turret wall. I want to be up there with them. I want to be ready to fight.

Aurus stands tall and proud, his feet planted on air. This is what he was born to do. The greatest Alpha, the High King of Ulfaria. Born to rule. Born to lead.

The bellies of the black ships open with a horrible creaking noise. The sulfuric odor pours out from them, making me gag. And something darts from one of the ships. Then more things—black, buzzing, shiny, in armored suits of their own.

The Chitin ships have their own warriors. And the enemy can also fly.

One buzzes overhead and I duck, even though it's hundreds of yards above me. It has beady black eyes, a horrible sort of mandible—it looks like a praying mantis, only jumbo sized. Human sized. Alpha sized.

The Chitin are some sort of bug. Huge, horrible, Alpha-sized alien bugs.

My skin crawls just looking at them. They're pouring from their ships in black swarms—hundreds upon hundreds, then thousands upon thousands of them.

And Aurus is just hanging out in midair, acting as if this is all normal. As the plague of Chitin swarms forward, he raises his hands higher, and flames shoot out of his gloves.

The Chitin make some sort of clicking sound—it's disgusting, and echoed a millionfold by their brethren. Sky cockroaches.

The Alpha soldiers blast forward in their flying suits, attacking the bugs with their built-in flame-throwers. Rank upon golden rank zooms in a triangular formation, cutting through the Chitin swarm.

Fire crackles. Smoking bugs fall from the sky. But there are so many Chitin, and so few Ulfarri warriors. They're just small flecks of gold in a seething black sky.

I need to help. I can't just stand here and watch. This may not be my planet, but... Fuck it. It *is* my planet. I may not be totally happy here, but I don't want it overrun by creepy alien bugs.

I need a weapon.

I run to the guardhouse wall. Where's the stupid button? Maybe there's another suit of armor I can use, or at least pry the gun away from.

I smack the wall's smooth surface. How did Emma figure this shit out?

Somehow, I press the right spot and another section of the wall opens. This time, a huge gun unfolds out of its hidden compartment.

Fuck yeah!

"Omega," someone shouts. It's a robed figure on the stairs. A Beta—one of the servants, his pale turquoise skin blanched with distress. "You should not be here! You must go down to safety!"

"We need to help them" I scream back.

"You cannot fight," the Beta fusses. "You are an Omega."

"I'm not just an Omega." I say. "I'm a badass." I push the gun with a grunt and shout over my shoulder, "Help me, or get out of the fucking way!"

The Beta tries to argue, but when he sees I'm going to drag this gun over to the turreted wall's edge, he gives up. He marches to the guardhouse and pushes another hidden button. A whole array of guns rises from the ground, perfectly aligned to shoot over the wall.

A laugh barks out of me. "Fuck yeah!"

I run up to one, and look for a way to aim.

There's a boom, and all the guns fire. I raise my hands to cover my ears before I realize the blast is already over.

The Beta looks smug. "Firebombs. They are robotically controlled. They will lock on to the Chitin, and take them out."

"But you can't just fire indiscriminately. There are Alphas out there. And the king."

"These are only the first shots," he acknowledges.

The bombs hit the first waves of bugs, and explode. Fire billows among their ranks. A few black bodies rain down, their wings in pieces. Ulfarri soldiers zoom between them, burning the rest of the bits to black dust.

The air fills with that hellish, sulfuric smell. The wind carries the stench. I cough when it hits my face. Each breath burns like I'm sucking in acid. Tiny knives are cutting the insides of my nostrils. I rub my nose.

"And now?" I ask. "There are still more of them."

"It's up to the Aurum Army now."

"Put this thing on manual control," I order, indicating the gun. "Now."

"I must program it to override—"

"Do it!" I scream. "Now!"

I swing the gun around and point it at a cluster of Chitin swarming a single Alpha soldier. I aim for the edges of the mass, and shoot a firebomb into them. It explodes. The blast knocks the warrior back, but the Chitin around it all catch fire and fall. The Alpha zooms away.

"Haha, yeah!" I punch the air.

"Well done," the Beta murmurs.

I grin at him. "I told you I'm a badass."

His face contorts; he's staring at something over my shoulder.

"What?" I whirl around. Crap, the Chitin must have realized something was shooting at them. A black cloud of them is coming our way.

"Run!" The Beta grabs me, and we dive for the stairwell. I land hard on the stone, covering my head with my hands.

Something zooms overhead.

"Look!" The Beta gasps.

I'm afraid to, but I peer out of the opening to the stairs as best I can while still keeping cover.

A ship hovers overhead. It's hardly bigger than a skimmer, with a triangular body and two long prongs sticking out in front. Red light crackles between the prongs. The ship's hull shimmers with a purplish sheen.

It darts forward, into the Chitin swarm. There's a crackling sound, and bits of bug start raining down. The stench of sulfur thickens, with an added bitter, burned edge.

Eww, fried bug.

Holding our hands over our mouths, the Beta and I take cover again.

"Who are they?" I shout through my fingers.

"Sky Fighters. The warriors of Altrim have come."

Altrim—Emma's kingdom. "Yes," I growl. "Get 'em, Khan. Fuck them up."

Purple ships zig-zag across the sky. They are smaller and faster than the Chitin spaceships, but bigger than the bugs. The red lasers make short work of the black cloud, and then the Sky Fighters cluster around the Chitin's ships. Red flashes pulse out of their purple hulls, slicing into the black craft. More obsidian bugs pour out of their spaceships, raining down upon the Sky Fighters.

But Aurus's warriors are ready, flying into the swarm like golden avenging angels. Between the Sky Fighters and the Aurum Army, the Chitin ranks begin to thin.

Both the Beta and I watch from our hiding place.

"Thanks for your help," I tell him. "I appreciate it. I'm Kim, by the way."

"I know." He looks down his narrow nose at me. "The Omega."

"Kim," I prompt. "I have a name."

"Kim. I am Terral." He purses his lips. "Is there a chance I can convince you to descend to the bunker?" he asks, and sighs when I shake my head. As soon as I can, I will return to the gun, but right now, the Sky Fighters have things covered.

"The Chitin," I say. "What are they?"

"An alien race from another galaxy. The Chitin have long been enemies of Ulfaria. They come to a planet, wipe out all life there, and use the barren soil to breed."

Gross. I wrinkle my nose. "Do they come often?"

"It has been years since the last attack—but we have not forgotten. We have crafted weapons and warning systems in the outer layer of our atmosphere, but it seems those satellites have failed. Now, our only hope is that the Alphas can stand against them. They are our final layer of defense."

I guess it's good that the Alphas grow so big.

"The warrior class has been bred over centuries," the Beta continues quietly. "They ensure Ulfaria's survival. Without Omegas, we cannot replace them."

I give him a sharp look, but he's watching the battle.

I sigh. I guess that's why this planet is obsessed with me breeding. I pick out Aurus's form from the rest of the fighters. He's leading the pack, a golden comet streaking across the sky.

"Be safe," I whisper. He might be an asshat, but he's *my* asshat. I don't want him to die.

Aurus

In-flight battles are infinitely complex. On the ground, the enemy can attack from the front, the rear, or the sides. In the air, they can also descend from above or ascend from below. Three-hundred-and-sixty-five degree points of attack... squared.

Fortunately, the warriors of Aurus are trained in air combat from a young age. And I was the youngest warrior of them all.

Fire weapons belch flames on all sides. The heat presses in. The air is a wall of charred dust and smoke. I don't hover so much as swim through the grey clouds.

Something clicks to my right. It's the clacking mandibles and wings of a Chitin. My arm shoots out and flames stream from the center of my gloved palm.

Our suits are cooling and fire resistant. The Chitin are tough, but not as tough as our armor. What they have in their favor are sheer numbers.

When we received alerts about the Chitin's potential arrival in our space, the Council of Kings convened. We were startled but not worried. Our planet has many layers of defense. In the past, the Alpha fighters were Ulfaria's only defense against the Chitin. Now, the magic tech we've developed in the past century can stop the Chitin from broaching our atmosphere.

However, it seems those advanced defenses have somehow failed. The Chitin should never have had the chance to get this close.

Either every single element of our defensive layers failed individually, or the Chitin have become more advanced since they last visited our galaxy. All of this is possible. But not likely.

That leaves another possibility: someone dismantled the alerts and our space defenses. Meaning this attack was orchestrated from within. By a traitor.

My roar reverberates in my helmet. I swoop into a black field of Chitin, taking them out with my flame. Bodies fall left and right.

A line of Sky Fighters screams overhead. Khan's forces are focused on attacking the Chitin spaceships—shooting them from all sides, breaking them apart. Locking on to the pieces and firing, disintegrating them into dust that will rain harmlessly onto Aurum. My people have practiced evacuating to bunkers until the attacks are over, and I declare the cities safe. If all goes to plan, the citizens of Aurum will survive this.

It's up to the Alphas now.

A whisper of Kim's scent flickers through my nostrils. I can sense her worry, her watchfulness. She is safe, but thinking of me.

The bond forming. A quiet swell of warmth blooms in my chest. I have no time to consider it, but I carry it with me all the same.

Clouds of Chitin billow out of the ship ahead of me. I zoom forward, fire weapon raised. I fight for my kingdom, for my people, but most of all for my Omega. For Kim.

She is the reason I must not only fight, but survive. She is the reason I must win.

Kim

The sky overhead is boiling with smoke. Bits and pieces of Chitin rain down on the palace in a clattering downpour.

It's deafening: the creepy clicking, the whoosh of flames, the crunch of wings and carapaces meeting armor—and thunder in the distance as the Chitin spaceships crash to the ground.

The tide of the battle is turning. A few Chitin ships ascend into the heights, trying to return to space. Sky Fighters hound them, red lightning striking their hulls again and again. Still, Sky Fighters and Aurum warriors have also fallen—streaking comets flaming bright through the enemy swarms as they hurtle from the sky.

"Come on," I shout to Terral, and race back out to the gun. I aim it at solitary clusters of Chitin, and fire upon the swarms. But I'm really watching the skies. Where is Aurus?

Finally, I spot him. He's hovering by a spaceship hull, incinerating Chitin at their source. A trio of Sky Fighters swoop at the huge ship, their lasers carving into its hull. It starts shaking. Aurus leans back, and zooms out of the way as it falls. But a huge cloud of insects hover, left by their mothership to die.

The Sky Fighters are gone, following the spaceship down, carving it into smaller pieces. That leaves only Aurus. Huge, gold, armored, armed—and alone. The perfect target.

I'm biting my lip hard. Aurus raises his arms, shooting flames into the enemy above him. Bits of Chitin start raining down on either side of him. Small flashes of gold wink at me through the seething shadow of the insects' bodies.

"No!" I try to aim, but I don't want to firebomb him. I've got to do something.

I leave my post, and dash for the skimmer.

"Kim!" Terral shouts. "What are you doing?"

"I've got to go to him." I grab the joystick, fingering the lump on my forehead with a wince. The last time I did this, it didn't end so well. Second time's the try?

"You cannot!" Terral grabs my ankle and tugs. I keep my hold on the joystick. I could kick him in the face—but I don't want to hurt him.

"I have to go," I cry. "He can't fight them all! There are too many!"

"He is the king! It is his right to fight, to die for us!"

"Not on my watch…" I twist out of Terral's grip. He overbalances and stumbles backwards, shock seizing his features.

I lean in to the joystick and lift off. The skimmer shoots away from the palace. I angle it to head towards the black cluster that's surrounding Aurus…

…just in time to watch his armored body plummet out of the bottom of the Chitin cloud, and continue to fall.

Aurus

My armor's systems are overloaded. The combination of dust and smoke is too much. The Chitin are directed by a hive mind, which makes them individually stupid. But they are hard to beat when they act as one, each individual sacrificing themselves for an overall victory.

Their main form of attack is to overwhelm an Aurum soldier, jam his suit's boosters, and let gravity do the rest.

Now, several are hovering in the air, ready to feast on my flesh when my body hurtles to the ground.

Not. Going. To. Happen. As my boosters fail, I angle myself backwards and spray fire into the hovering swarm. If I die, I'll take as many as I can out with me.

I have fought the good fight. I have given my all. For my kingdom. For my people.

My one regret is that I will leave behind my one and only love. My Kim—

"LEEEROOOYYYYY JENKINS!" A fierce cry pierces the air. I twist, my mouth open. There's Kim, her short hair plastered to her head in the whistling wind, her green eyes wide, and lips stretched with maniacal glee.

"No!" I roar, trying to wave her away a second before I slam onto the skimmer. The platform bucks under my weight, and Kim's slight body jerks wildly back and forth.

"Whoa!" Only her grip on the controller keeps her from falling off. "Hang on, big guy!" She zooms up, down, around a swarm, then onward into a patch of clear sky, cackling the whole time.

"What are you doing!" I bellow, holding on to the side of the skimmer. This thing is a pleasure craft, not made for warfare. That point is proven when the craft tips in an evasive maneuver, and I promptly topple off it.

"Crap!" Kim shouts, whipping the skimmer around to catch me. I punch through a few Chitin, smashing their wings and incinerating what I can before I land with a thud on the platform once more.

"Kim!" I'm livid, my blood boiling.

"Sorry! This thing is wild. Like a magic carpet ride... should I sing the song? A whole new wooorld—AHHH!"

The Chitin are racing after us, a seething, clicking monster made up of many bodies in flight. Just as they're gaining on us, Kim accidentally twists the joystick in the wrong direction. We shoot backwards. The Chitin scatter.

"Whoops!" Kim squeaks, and shifts the controller. The skimmer shudders left, right, up, and down. "This thing is sensitive, isn't it? Like giving a handjob... good thing I'm good with those, right?"

We plummet thirty feet, leaving my heart and stomach hovering in the clouds above us.

"Get us back to the palace," I roar.

"Fine," she grumbles. "You don't want to fight up here anymore?"

"NOW!"

The skimmer continues to drop, shuddering to a halt a few times as Kim figures out how to descend properly. The jerky drop bounces me against the platform over and over. I bite my lip to keep from shouting at her. She's doing the best she can.

She was supposed to be in the bunker, safe. I could kill her for doing this... but...

She came for me. And she saved my life.

As long as she doesn't kill us both by crashing the skimmer. We're not safe yet.

She overshoots the tower. A small, robed figure stands atop it, waving wildly. As we pass, I recognize him—it's Terral. The Beta watches us zoom past, then rushes to man the guns and shoot down anyone following us.

The skimmer scrapes over the top of a wall, toppling a statue of a long-dead Alpha warrior. The platform tilts, and I grab for the side as I begin to slide off it. The arena is below us. The pink sandy ground is rapidly approaching, along with the dais and the wooden structure holding up the Gong of Honor.

"Aurus!" Kim shrieks. The skimmer hits the sand and

starts sliding. The gong and platform loom closer. We're going to crash—

Bong!

Kim

There's a deafening ringing in my ears, but other than that, I'm fine. I crashed the skimmer—again—but luckily, it had slowed enough beforehand for us not to be seriously hurt. Good thing I hit that statue on the way in.

To my right, Aurus is lying in a pile of dented armor. For a moment, I feel a flicker of concern, then he groans and sits up slowly. It would take more than a wild ride on a skimmer to kill him.

And what a wild ride it was.

"That was awesome!" I'm out of breath, laughing. I fucking did it. I saved Aurus, and landed us in the arena. Okay, so it could have been more graceful, but that will come in time. The skimmer lies in scattered pieces on the sand. We hit something... oh. The gong. So that's what that ringing noise was. Is. The gong is embedded in the wall a few yards away, still quivering. The wooden frame that held it up is in splinters, and the dais it was on did not survive.

But we did.

Adrenaline zings through my veins. I want to run around the arena, crowing. No wonder the Alphas love to fight! It's fucking awesome.

"Kim!" A roar, and Aurus is on me. His huge body covers me, pinning me to the sand. I get a face full of enraged Alpha.

His teeth are bared, his dark amber eyes wild.

"What were you doing? Why did you risk your life?" He sits up, pulling me into his lap, then shakes me. "Did you even stop to think?"

What the fuck? I just saved this asshat's life! "I had to do something!" I clutch his arms to steady myself, and yell right back into his face. "Everyone was helping—I wanted to help!"

"You were supposed to stay safe!" His roar blasts my hair back.

"While aliens tried to destroy us? I don't think so."

"Ulf, Kim." He's so furious, his arms are trembling. He releases me to push a hand through his hair, clutching his head as he mutters, "You cannot do this to me."

"Do what?" I snarl.

"Play games with your life."

I'm about to snap back that none of this was a game when he stops, and starts to pant like he's having a heart attack.

"I cannot... cannot..." He bares his teeth, looking pained, as if this whole conversation is giving him a headache. Deep furrows line his golden brow.

"Can't what?"

His head droops, and his eyes close for a moment. His lips are moving, and I lean closer to make out what he's saying. The battle in the sky is still going on, off in the distance, but the smoke and sounds are suddenly far away.

There's just me and Aurus in a cocoon of our own making, and our shared breaths.

"I cannot... lose you."

"Why?" I can't keep the bitter edge out of my voice. "Because I'm your perfect little Omega?"

"No," he growls, and gives me another hard shake. There's a pause. "Because you are my everything."

His fingertips are digging into my arms so hard they might leave bruises—but I barely register the pain. My heart is hammering in my chest. "What?"

"Kim..." He strokes a trembling hand over my cheek, the panic in his expression starting to fade. "You must understand. Do you realize what would happen if I lost you?"

"You'd have to get another Omega?"

He shakes his head. He cups my face, his tender expression making my breath catch. "No. No." His gaze pins me. Each word comes out like it weighs a millstone. "I would not survive your loss."

I'm not sure I heard right. It feels like my heart is trying to leap from my chest.

"Kim. You must understand." His thumbs stroke my cheeks, his fingers questing deeper into my hair. "You are my other half. You are my soul. You. Are. My. Everything."

I forget to breathe as I stare at his handsome face, absorbing his statement, trying to see whether he's telling the truth.

His gaze is fathomless, his very soul bared to me.

He meant it—every word.

The joy rising up in my chest is unlike anything I've ever felt. With a cry, I launch myself at him. He hoists me up, meeting my mouth with his. Our lips lock in a kiss both fierce and tender. My hands are frantic, pulling him against me. His chuckle is muffled by our kiss and I nip at his lips, wanting to punish him for thinking this is funny.

His growl reverberates through us both. I wrap my legs around his waist, locking my ankles behind him, my pussy aching with a sudden, clawing desire. I need him inside me. Now.

He tears at my already tattered dress. Bits of fabric flutter to the ground.

Slowly, he lies back, bringing me with him. I end up straddling him, rubbing my slick sex over the hard bar of his cock.

He bares his teeth. "You are never to follow me into battle again."

"You were fighting—you almost died," I counter, still rubbing myself against him. "You think I could just stand by and watch that happen?"

"You must. You are too precious to me. You cannot fight —I forbid it!"

He tries to grip my hair, but the strands are so short, I can duck my head away easily. "You can't stop me from being who I am," I mutter.

"Ulfdammit!" he roars, and rolls, pinning me under him, his huge hand clamping down over both my wrists. "I will lock you in my quarters. I will chain you to my bed."

"And I'll pick the lock," I say smugly, if a bit breathlessly. "And then I'll chain *you* up. Let's see how you like it, asshat."

"You can try."

"You will fail."

He groans, dropping his head and pressing his lips to the tender place where my neck meets my shoulder. The wound throbs with a delicious ache. "I love you so much."

Warmth blooms through me. My heart feels like it might burst. "I hate you... only a little." I'm fighting the smile on my face. "Less every day."

"I will earn your love," he vows. His huge hand skims the underside of my leg, hooking my knee and cocking it high. My drenched pussy opens to him, and his hard cock is right there, nudging the entrance.

I shiver and wriggle as he pushes inside, stretching me.

He stills, and I turn my head and nip his arm to punish him for going too slowly. I can't wait any longer.

He groans and seats himself fully between my legs, the familiar burning ache searing my sex. "My Omega."

"My Alpha," I counter, growling. "Mine."

"Do you hate me now?" He gives a hard thrust.

"Yes...." I pant, a wave of pleasure rolling up my groin. "Maybe..."

"How about now?" He swivels his hips, catching my clit. I close my eyes, my pussy clenching as the sensation throbs all the way through me.

It's a while before I can answer. "A little less. Keep going. It's helping." I sound like I'm drunk.

I free my hands, and dig my nails into his back. His knot is already swelling, joining us together. There is nothing like sex with Aurus.

Nothing.

For a while, nothing exists but the push and pull of our bodies, the grunts and groans and shudders as we lose ourselves in each other.

When we're sated, I'm lying limply beneath him on the sand, staring up at the smoke-streaked sky, with an enormous grin on my face. There's a warmth in my heart—a subtle, flickering flame. It matches the heat in my loins, but somehow, I know this heart fire will last longer.

The desperate heat of my estrus is already fading. That's the good thing about the IUD. It seems to suppress the Omega serum just enough.

One day, I'll secretly get the *magicians* to remove it. I'll let the heat come, and jump Aurus. It will be a hell of a surprise for him.

Until then, I like my estrus as it is. Short and sweet.

After all, I've got things to do. Courtesans to empower. Skimmers to pilot. Battles to win.

Aurus is rubbing his head against mine, his scent coating my skin and filling my chest. "I love your hair," he mumbles.

"Really?"

"Mmm."

I push at his chest, trying to prop myself up. His knot is already softening, his cock slipping out of me. "I thought you hated it."

He lets out a huff. "I did—at first. But now, I can't imagine it any other way. You are so different... my little warrior."

My grin widens. Aurus sounds as drunk as I feel. "Who're you calling little?" I feign indignation.

"You. You are so small." He captures my wrist, and kisses my palm. His tongue flicks the center before I snatch my hand away. If he starts licking me, I'm going to want to lick him... and do other things. And we have places to be.

"Only compared to you." I make a fist, and punch his enormous bicep. He pretends to roar in pain, and I laugh because it's so obviously fake.

He drops his hips back down, pinning my hands to the sand when I pretend to struggle. I sigh as his weight settles on me. This is perfection.

"No," Aurus says. "You are not the Omega I expected."

I bite my lip. I'm getting sick of hearing that.

He rubs his cheek against mine, and leans back to spear me with his amber gaze. "But Kim, you are exactly what I needed."

I swallow against my suddenly hard throat. "Really?"

"You are everything I didn't know I could want. Better that I could have imagined... or dreamed of."

A tremor goes through me, and my eyes are suddenly wet. Dammit, I'm getting all gushy. Who knew I was longing to hear my big golden asshat tell me this? "I'm never going to be a sweet, submissive courtesan," I warn, blinking furiously. "I'm not the type."

"You're sweet with me," he purrs, nuzzling my neck. He licks the bite, and a jolt of achy pleasure rushes through me. My limbs feel weak. In another second, I'll be helpless to resist, so I swat him. "Stop it."

He captures my offending hand and kisses it. "You are submissive when you take my cock."

"Stop it," I huff. I'm getting super wet again. "You know what I mean. I'm not all cultured and refined." I mime drinking tea with my pinky finger sticking out, which is stupid because Aurus probably has no idea what a teacup is.

"You are perfect."

I open my mouth to argue but close it again. After all, why would I argue with that? "Go on..."

"You are beautiful and wise. A strong and able—if tiny—warrior."

"And I stand up to you," I add with a wink. "God knows you need it."

"I do not agree with that."

I snicker.

"You are perfect for me. My strong little Omega. My queen."

A purple Sky Fighter streaks over the arena, wind whistling in its wake. Sand gusts around us. We curl into each other, protecting our faces with each other's bodies.

When the gust has died down and the sand has settled, Aurus raises his head to peer at the sky.

"The battle is over," he says. "I must go."

I moan a little as his delicious weight leaves me. I roll up to sit, shaking sand from my hair, brushing it with my fingers. "Where are you going?"

"I am the king. I must see that my people are well, and put the kingdom back to rights." He turns to the broken skimmer and, with a rueful shake of his head, pivots away. He kicks aside his dented helmet as he strides for the exit.

It takes me a second to leap to my feet, but only because I'm too busy drooling over his sleekly muscled backside outlined in his breeches.

"Wait!" I dash after him. He slows, and I skid on the sand to a stop in front of him. "I'm going with you."

He opens his mouth to argue, and I point a finger right in his face. "You just told me I'm your queen. Does a queen lounge in a palace while her people are hurting? Or does she go and help?"

He glares at me.

I glare back. "Think carefully before you answer." My growl is as intimidating as any Alpha's.

"I wish you would stay here," he grumbles. "It may be dangerous."

"You'll keep me safe. And I'll protect you. We have each other's back. That's what being equals in a relationship means."

"Very well, my Kim." He caresses my cheek. "But first we will stop in our quarters for some fresh clothes."

"Deal." It's a good thing I already modified all my long gowns into something more practical.

There's a blooming warmth in my chest, unfolding its petals, blossoming bigger and bigger... until my entire being is basking in the perfect contentment of my heart. It's deeper and sweeter than mere happiness. Heavy and light at the same time.

I press my hand between my breasts. "I feel... is this the soul bond?"

"Yes." Aurus leans down so we're face to face. "Yes, that's it, my love."

Love. That's what this is. Emma was right. It does feel just like coming home. "I feel it," I whisper.

"I feel it too." His large hand covers mine. His fingers stroke mine with infinite gentleness. "I thought you didn't want the bond?"

"It's not so bad," I admit.

"No?"

"I can live with it," I say breezily, deciding I've had enough of this touchy feely stuff. "Now, let's go." I push at his heavy shoulder. "Your people are waiting." I want to make sure the Beta ladies—Juno, Lenah and the rest—are all okay in the city.

"Yes, little queen." He straightens. "But afterwards..." His cock prods my side, hard and heavy. He could club a Chitin with that thing.

"Absolutely." I grin. "We'll go and change, and then the first one to the skimmer gets to drive!" I take off towards the entrance to the palace, Aurus's roar following me.

"No! Kim! Stop!" He tries to run, but his huge erection must be slowing him down. "You little—"

The last of his shout is drowned out by my cackle. I enter the palace and run round the corner but I can still feel him through the soul bond: his frustration, his arousal—and, even deeper than his strong desire, his love.

He'll be with me, always. And I'll be with him.

Forever.

EPILOGUE

Kim

"My queen." A deep voice rings out over the sand.

I turn from the practice dummy I've been whaling on.

Aurus is striding across the arena towards me. "I thought I'd find you here."

"Hey there," I call, setting down my sword. I need a break, anyway. My arms are trembling from the exertion of practicing my side cuts.

I wrench off my helmet and cock my head. My short hair is probably sticking up all over the place, but that's okay. Now that Aurus is used to my shaggy pixie cut, he seems to adore it. "Have you come to best me?"

"Perhaps later..." His gaze wanders down over my form, and hungry flames flicker in his eyes.

In the hours after the Chitin attack, Aurus and I were truly a team. We flew all over Aurum, giving aid, directing the Alphas. I got to visit with the former courtesans, who are happily living in their new houses in the city. Aurus introduced me to the kingdom's magistrates and his people as their new queen.

Weeks passed, and slowly the kingdom and palace life returned to normal. I was afraid Aurus would go back to his old ways. One morning, I woke up alone and thought my fears had been confirmed.

Then the doors opened and Aurus was standing there, presenting me with proof of his devotion: a whole array of weapons and fighting gear—even including a Kim-sized set of armor, modified especially for me. When I wear it, I look like a mini Alpha. The first time I put it on, Aurus thought I was so cute, he burst out laughing. I used the distraction to my advantage, and whacked him with a wooden training sword.

I almost won that fight. I'm getting better at sparring, now that Aurus is training me. I spend most of my free time practicing.

My favorite pastime, of course, is sparring with Aurus before bed. We do it naked. I have no idea who wins those matches—mostly because, after my fourth or fifth orgasm, I no longer care.

"Are you sure?" I press. "If you win... I'll do a sexy striptease. If I win, I get my very own skimmer."

"Absolutely not."

"Then you have to best me, fair and square..." I start stripping off my armor. Maybe I can distract him with my body, and win that way.

For a moment, it works... then he blinks, and shakes his head, visibly getting himself back under control. "I have news."

I lay down my breastplate. "Good news?"

"Of a sort. Come." He takes a seat on the newly rebuilt dais, and holds out a hand. I roll my eyes but practically skip over to him. He's still bossy as ever. That's okay. I kind of like it.

"I have just come from a meeting with Khan," he announces. "We have made a decision about the Omega program."

Oh. I bite my lip. "Okay." I brace myself.

"We're pausing the program until we can find a way to screen the humans we take."

"What? Really?" I had hardly dared to hope that Khan and Aurus would listen to us when Emma and I listed our concerns.

"Yes." He runs a hand over my head, almost like he's petting me. But I don't hate it. I push my head against his shoulder and nuzzle, letting him stroke me. "The other kings will not like it, but it is the best way."

I climb into his lap and cup his face. "Thank you. And thank Khan, too." I can't wait to discuss this with Emma. "This means a lot to us." And to the human women who won't be abducted. Emma and I are happy here, but we want women to have a choice.

I brush my lips against his, ready to show how happy I am. He kisses me but leans back, his face somber.

"I have more news, however. About the Chitin attack. The engineers have catalogued the rubble, and in doing so, they found some plans detailing information that should not have been in their possession. It seems the enemy had coordinates to help them locate our palace and the capital city of Aurum. What's more, there was evidence of a comms transmission from our planet to their ships."

I blink, my mind reeling, trying to sort out what Aurus is saying. "What does that mean?"

"Someone was in communication with the Chitin. Someone here, on Ulfaria. The same someone—Khan and I believe—who tampered with our defenses to allow the Chitin to enter our atmosphere."

"Holy crap," I breathe. "The attack was an inside job? But why?" Who on Ulfaria would want the Chitin to attack their own planet?

"Our best guess is that the Chitin's attack was not an attack on Aurum. It was a diversion."

This is some next level conspiracy shit. "To distract from what?"

"During the attack, there was a disruption in the magicians' towers. One of the magicians appears to have stolen secret information. He killed several of his brethren, and fled. Now he's nowhere to be found."

"What did he steal?"

"Amongst other things, the Omega serum." Aurus strokes his hand over my head again. "Kim, it gets worse. We believe he's already opened a portal and brought over more Hoo-mans and injected them with the serum. They might be here on Ulfaria as we speak."

My blood freezes and burns at the same time. "Oh, fuck." Horrified, I clap a hand over my mouth. "We have to find them..."

"Yes, of course." Aurus looks grim. "We will be on the lookout. But we have to be careful to search without alerting all the kings."

"Wait, why?"

"Because they will stop at nothing to find the Omegas first. And when they find them..."

Shit. The answer is as obvious as it is terrifying. "They'll claim them."

He nods, gravely. "And there will be nothing we can do."

Haley

I'm having the strangest dream. I'm lying on some kind of dewy lawn, with moisture seeping into my skin from below. There's what looks like a fern leaf brushing my face. It's nighttime but the sky is bright with the light of the moon. No—*five* moons. Five? What the fuck?

I run a hand over my head and my fingers get snagged. My hair is tangled from sleep. Something bites my bare thigh sharply, and I swat it, but miss. Some sort of lightning bug zooms away—but it's bigger and more wicked-looking than any insect I've ever seen before. And it was bright red. Definitely unlike any lightning bug I've ever seen.

I rub my leg. Whatever it was, that thing bit me, and it really hurt. Which sucks, but what sucks even more is what the sharp pinch didn't do.

It didn't wake me up.

Which means, I'm already awake.

This isn't a dream. This is really happening to me.

Where am I?

I sit up, my damp limbs aching, trying to get my bearings. There's a relentless pounding in my skull, and a bitter taste in my mouth. I wish I had something cold to drink.

A branch cracks, and I whirl around, my heart suddenly hammering in my chest. A ghostly shape pushes her way through the brush, and staggers to a stop next to me. She looks exhausted.

"Ulf," she exclaims in a high-pitched voice. The newcomer's wearing a pale, flimsy-looking robe that brushes the tops of her thighs. And nothing else. The robe is pretty see-through.

The woman pushes back her long hair to gape at me. Her eyes are a bit too big for her face. And her ears... have pointed tips. Like an elf's.

Maybe I'm at some sort of costume party... and I drank too much? That would explain my woozy head. But that wouldn't explain why she doesn't sound like she's speaking English.

"Um," I manage. My lips feel too big for my face.

Before I can ask where I am and what I'm doing here, the woman leans in, her huge eyes wide.

"What are you doing?" she hisses. "You can't stay here! The Alphas are coming! We must run!" Reaching down, she grabs my hand, wraps long, slender fingers around my wrist, and pulls me into the night.

One click Brutal Capture now...

EXCLUSIVE BONUS VERY SHORT STORY!

Want more Kim and Aurus? Sign up to the Planet of Kings newsletter HERE (https://geni.us/Alphagift) and get a special bonus novella which is not available anywhere else!

What do you give a King who has everything? Kim has an idea...

WANT MORE PLANET OF KINGS?

Brutal Mate - Emma & Khan's story
Brutal Claim - Kim & Aurus' story
Brutal Capture - Haley & The Hunter King
Brutal Beast - Rose & The Beast King

A Gift for the Alpha - very short bonus novella starring Kim & Aurus with cameos of Emma & Khan

You can sign up to receive the story for FREE here: https://geni.us/Alphagift

TABITHA BLACK

USA Today bestselling author Tabitha Black loves to write steamy books featuring growly, dominant Alphas and the women who love them. Her latest forays are into dark paranormal romance, including the deliciously hot world of M/f Omegaverse.

She has a weakness for great coffee, strong, dominant men, and tattoos.

Tabitha loves getting mail, so if you want to drop her a line, please do so at tabitha_black@hotmail.com. You can also sign up for her newsletter, follow her on BookBub, or join her Facebook page. Thank you for reading!

Don't miss these other exciting books by Tabitha Black!

Contemporary

His Empire Series
Restraint - Book 1
Denial - Book 2
Anticipation - Novella

Masters of the Castle Series
Fulfilling Her Fantasy
Sharing Silver
Tempting Tasha
Undoing Una

Midnight Doms
Her Vampire Addiction

Anthologies
When the Gavel Falls (Sharing Silver)
Witness Protection Program (Tempting Tasha)
Dominating His Valentine (Anticipation)
Daddies of the Castle (Undoing Una)

Paranormal

Alphas of Sandor
Primal Possession - Book 1
Primal Mate - Book 2

Planet of Kings - With Lee Savino
Brutal Mate - Book 1
Brutal Claim - Book 2
Brutal Capture - Book 3 (available Feb 2022)

Audiobooks
Little Tudor Rose
Conquering Cassia
Restraint
Sapphire's Surrender
Primal Possession

ABOUT LEE SAVINO

Lee Savino is a USA today bestselling author of smexy romance. Smexy, as in "smart and sexy." Find her in the Goddess Group on facebook and download a free book at www.leesavino.com!

Find her at:
www.leesavino.com

Want more growly alphas? Check out the Berserker Saga. Start with Sold to the Berserkers.

Remember to download your free book at www.leesavino.com

The Berserker Saga

Sold to the Berserkers – Brenna, Samuel & Daegan
Mated to the Berserkers - – Brenna, Samuel & Daegan
Bred by the Berserkers (FREE novella only available at www.leesavino.com) - – Brenna, Samuel & Daegan
Taken by the Berserkers – Sabine, Ragnvald & Maddox
Given to the Berserkers – Muriel and her mates
Claimed by the Berserkers – Fleur and her mates

Ménage Sci Fi Romance

Draekons (Dragons in Exile) with Lili Zander (ménage alien dragons)

Crashed spaceship. Prison planet. Two big, hulking, bronzed aliens who turn into dragons. The best part? The dragons insist I'm their mate.

Paranormal romance

Bad Boy Alphas with Renee Rose (bad boy werewolves)
Never ever date a werewolf.

Possessive Warrior Sci fi romance

Draekon Rebel Force with Lili Zander
Start with Draekon Warrior

Tsenturion Warriors with Golden Angel
Start with Alien Captive

Contemporary Romance

Royal Bad Boy
I'm not falling in love with my arrogant, annoying, sex god boss. Nope. No way.

Royally Fake Fiancé
The Duke of New Arcadia has an image problem only a fiancé can fix. And I'm the lucky lady he's chosen to play Cinderella.

Beauty & The Lumberjacks

After this logging season, I'm giving up sex. For...reasons.

Her Marine Daddy
My hot Marine hero wants me to call him daddy...

Her Dueling Daddies
Two daddies are better than one.

Innocence: dark mafia romance with Stasia Black
I'm the king of the criminal underworld. I always get what I want. And she is my obsession.

Beauty's Beast: a dark romance with Stasia Black
Years ago, Daphne's father stole from me. Now it's time for her to pay her family's debt...with her body.

Printed in Great Britain
by Amazon